YA BOOKS   REALMS OF TIME

IGNITED   *AWAKEN THE FLAMES*

Suspense/Thrillers

MINE

AWAKEN

THE FLAMES

By Ryenn Ginger

AWAKEN THE FLAMES

ISBM-13: 9798707101670 (paperback)

For

F.C who told me to release this years ago

(I finally listened to you)

&

R.L. Who let me bounce my crazy idea's

amid candy filled conversations

PROLOGUE

Scared, alone wandering the streets aimlessly wondering why she couldn't remember things. As if a large part of her life was wiped out, someone was tampering with forces beyond their control. Being pregnant, that much was obvious to her, but she couldn't recall who the father was. Lucia said she would help protect her, but even Nina had her doubts. Whoever was after her didn't know about the child she carried and she'd keep it that way.

Knowing her friend would keep her secret, against all else she trusted her in that. For now, however, Nina had to keep the baby safe; jumping between realms wasn't an option anymore, she couldn't risk it. The throne could wait, hell her brother could have it if he wanted, she never wanted that life anyway. He was the last person that she would trust, but his help leaving the realm would be imperative. She had to keep her daughter safe.

With the labor pains growing stronger, Nina couldn't wait. The pain mounting, she wasn't left with a choice. Appearing at the hospital as quickly as she could, a sweet nurse came to her aid. The girl's heart was pure, Nina could feel it; there was something special about her and she'd play an important part in her child's life.

Seeing the woman appear from nowhere Mary knew that something was wrong. Sensing magic at work, she had to help. Who or whatever she was, she was taking a risk having the baby in a mortal hospital? The child was a witch-ling she carried, and by the look on her face Mary didn't think she even knew. She could feel the cloak of magic swirling around her, someone didn't want her found.

The baby was radiating power and it wasn't even born yet. Mary knew that she would do whatever it would take to keep them safe; whoever had hidden her did it for a reason. Feeling the energy around her vibrate with power as the new life sprung into the world, Mary made a vow to protect them from whatever the future held.

Looking upon the beautiful baby girl she brought into the world, Nina's heart melted.

This little life brought her so much joy in a single moment, she would bottle the happiness for a

lifetime. Holding Adrianna close to her chest, Nina felt whole again. That piece

of her heart that was missing was filled once more. She would deal with her daughter's

questions about her father years from now, and maybe as the years go by, she will remember.

Ensuring that there was no one around, with Adrianna bundled in her arms Nina jumped quickly to her realm, knowing exactly where to find her friend. There sitting on the stone bench in the garden was Lucia, the wind gracefully playing with her hair. Taking the seat beside her, she placed Adrianna in her arms.

"She's stunning Nina, you have a darling baby girl."

"Yes, Lucia she is beautiful, and special as well, she will one day be princess of this world."

"This child is special Nina, more than you know. Now quickly, take her and leave, your brother is coming and he doesn't need to know about her yet, in a few years maybe. I'll send word when he is not around so you can visit. Now go! Quickly!" Placing Adrianna back in Nina's arms Lucia knew exactly who the child was. The prince didn't need to know about her yet, for her own safety.

Placing a kiss on the baby's head, Lucia quickly gave her friend a hug and watched as they vanished from sight. Feeling the shift in the air as he drew closer, as if the wind was retreating from his path, the prince was no one to be messed with.

"Lucia, who were you talking to?"

"No one. Why do you ask?"

"I thought I heard my sisters voice."

"Your sister has been gone for years. You have gotten what you wanted, her out of the picture."

"Well, once she's no longer a threat to me, I will feel a whole lot better."

"You're truly a pathetic man, you do know that." Egging him on wasn't good. Knowing she had gone too far. Silently calling the wind to keep her safe, she knew she was protected.

"Your powers can only keep you safe for so long Lucia. There will be a time when it won't

work for you. My sister may have convinced our parent to ensure your safety, but when I'm

king, it won't save you."

"When your king, all will truly be lost. You sister will come home one day."

"She's lost and confused and will stay that way for a very long time."

Leaving Lucia in the garden, he needed to make a stop. He flashed to meet with an

old friend. One he left very specific instruction for. She was just as power hungry as he was.

The only difference, she was a witch, and he made sure that she saw her mother suffer. Only he

was the cause behind it not her father? But that didn't matter, as long as the end result was the

same.

"Serina, did you do what I asked?"

"Yes, she's gone and won't remember a thing. That I promise. She'll be tormented by

memories of a man, but never see his face."

"Great, everything is working out wonderfully."

"About my payment? I did what you asked."

"You'll get your payment when the time is right. Now leave. Make a life far away from here.

You will know when it's time to return. Not a trace until then. By the way, how's that brother

of yours." Smirking he knew that her brother could hear everything.

CHAPTER ONE

A sharp knock on the front door had Adrianna tumbling out of bed in a mess of blankets and sheets. With four thirty flashing on the alarm, she could feel the frustration mounting. Waking up in the middle of the night wasn't high up on her list of favorite things to do. Wrapping the blanket around her, heading to confront whoever it was. Tightly clasping the material around her shoulders; peering out the eye hole.

Her uncle was standing on the front step, hands clasped, his head tilted slightly down shielding his face from the light of the moon. There was something about him that always kept her uneasy. Years had passed since she'd seen him and the same feeling remained. He couldn't be trusted. Why her mother kept speaking to him she would never understand. Opening the door just enough to talk; still keeping her hand on it so closing it could be easy.

"What are you doing here?"

"Your mother called me last night, she wasn't well. I picked her up and took her to the hospital."

"What are you talking about? She's in bed, what's your problem anyway?"

"Adrianna, listen to me…."

1

"I've heard enough from you. What I don't understand is why you can't just stay away from her." Attempting to close the door before his foot blocked its path.

"She's not here Adrianna, go check for yourself." Arrogance radiating from him.

There was a flash in his eyes that made her question his actions. He wasn't her favorite person, but why was he here at this hour? Backing up, hesitantly letting him enter their home. Watching as he removed the fedora that he always wore resting it on the shelf by the door, something seemed to catch his eye, as a sneer crossed his face.

"Go. Look. She's not here." His voice dripped with smugness.

"Fine, I'll go. Prove you wrong, then you can leave and get on with your self-indulgent miserable life and leave us alone. Why my mom tolerates you I have no idea."

Turning to leave him, feeling her heart beat slowing with each step she took. Every footfall seeming like a thousand, something was wrong. Deep down unease crept over her. This was all a dream, repeating over again in her head. Reaching for the handle, stopping, pulling back ever so slightly. Turning to face him at the end of the hall.

Rocking on her heel before taking the first step, clasping the handle, squeezing her eyes closed for a moment. Pushing the door open, only to see her mothers' room empty, abandoned. Where was her mother?

"Where is she?" Anger rose, the pit of her stomach turning with confusion. "What have you done this time? Why can't you just let us be happy?" Adrianna screamed the words as she stormed to where she left him. "You could never just leave us alone, could you? Could you?" Tears streaming down her face as she pounded restlessly against his chest, each blow bouncing off as if she were a child hitting a balloon, he was completely unaffected, only driving her to hit harder.

"She passed away about an hour ago. She didn't want you to know, to see her like that."

"Like what? What are you talking about?"

"She'd been sick, had been for a while. She didn't want you to know."

"You're lying!" Taking a step back to get a better look at him. Her hatred growing by the second, there was something in his expression, something she never seen before. Reality began to sink in.

Her mother hadn't been herself for a while, just kept saying she was tired, or had a cold. Why didn't she push for more, get her to see a doctor? As if stoking a fire, she could feel the questions burning in her.

"I'm not lying hun, deep down you know it."

"Don't call me hun, and tell me what's going on." Hurt and anger radiating from her.

Feeling a soft hand slipping into hers giving it a gentle squeeze, she knew that Mary had come; she must have heard the arguing from next door. Adrianna needed answers, needed to stay focused.

"He's not lying Ad, I was with you mother when she passed, I agreed to allow him to tell you, but was never far away."

"What? What happened Mary? What happened to my mom?" Water clouding her sights as tears cascaded down her cheeks.

"Ok, let's sit down and I'll explain everything."

Sitting there listening in shock, realizing that her entire life had been a lie. How could she not know that her mother was sick? Why had they kept her in the dark? Hollowness began filling Adrianna, her mothers' attempt at protection left only more questions. Her mother had been sick for over a year, she never knew why. The doctors couldn't find a cause or reason. She did everything while Adrianna was at school, working or sleeping. There was never a night job that kept her mom tired. So many lies Adrianna couldn't fathom them.

Mary would take her to all the appointments. She did the cooking and cleaning, everything. Adrianna owed Mary her thanks for helping her mother, why was her uncle involved? She didn't buy that it was because her mother wanted there to be peace before she passed away.

Seeing that Adrianna needed some time, a quick glance from Mary had her uncle excusing himself to make a few calls; apparently her mother had arranged everything. As he left, she hoped that after the funeral she wouldn't have to see him again. Closing the door behind him, Mary made her way to the couch to join Adrianna. Not saying a word, she just sat there next to her.

Adrianna respected that, her house of cards was coming crashing down, trying to absorb everything she'd learned in such a short time. Her chest tightening, a burning feeling flowing through her veins, she could survive this, she just needed time.

Adrianna's face warmed, as the sunlight filtered through the curtains hit her face, unaware of how long she had been sitting there for. Her face stained from the tears, that had since dried up the night before. Seeing Mary steadfast sitting beside her, she was grateful her friend never left her side. As anger and hurt diminished, emptiness crept in.

So much had happened in the course of hours; her mother was gone, no longer of this world. She was alone, an orphan, no family. Her uncle didn't count. If a century went by it wouldn't be long enough, she thought. He had caused enough pain to last a life time. Adrianna's mother always tried to protect her from him. Why in the last year she had reached out she wouldn't understand. One day the answers would come, until then she would wait.

Sitting alone by her mothers' grave, so many questions lingered. Over the days more had arisen, than been answered. Leaning down, Adrianna placed her hand on the smooth finish of the casket, placing a single white daisy on top, closing her eyes, with a deep breath standing she turned to leave. Seeing her uncle in the distance, a smirk crossed over his lips. She'd deal with him later. Searching Mary out in the crowd it was time to go. A new life was going to start, and it wasn't one Adrianna was looking forward too.

Needing time to process everything that shattered her world in a moment. She needed to escape, but knew that Mary would never let her go far. The cool breeze through the trees helped ease the tension from my uncles' visit. It didn't sit well. Deciding I'll tell Mary when she gets home. Then at least she won't let him in. If he ever shows up again. Main Street wasn't a far walk. Coffee and book sounded good at the moment. Escaping to a different time and world was needed.

Watching as the summer baskets were being hung from the lamp posts. Their colors adding to the small-town feel. The street already busy with people escaping work for lunch. Always lots of people on nice days. The aroma of coffee on the wind, calling me forward. Lost in my thoughts, my hand brushed someone's as I reached for the door.

"Sorry. I wasn't paying attention. Go ahead."

"No, you first."

Peering from under her sunglasses. Turning. Hesitating. Their hands still touching. A surge of energy passed between them. His gaze, capturing her soul. Pulled into the soft emerald depths of his eyes. Time stood still, each passing second felt like an eternity. A lifetime of knowledge locked within. Her thick lashes lowered, hiding them from view. Shaking her head, bringing herself back to reality. What the hell had just happened?

Their hands slowly slipped apart. His lips curved into a devilish smile. The chatter of girls across the street pulled me back to reality.

"Thanks." The only words to escape me.

"My pleasure." A wink and a smile, as he held the door, allowing me to go inside.

"Sorry about that. It's been a bad day. I didn't notice you, kind of lost in my thoughts today."

"Happens. All good."

Holding the strap of her bag, for support. Heat crept into her face. Blushing? Really? As if she had time for that right now Adrianna thought to herself.

"You can go ahead. I don't know what I want yet." Staring aimlessly at the board. It wasn't like the order would ever change. The owner across the counter gave me a look. She knew what I'd ask for. It was always the same.

"You sure?"

"Ya."

"Thanks."

Listening as he placed his order. The sounds of his voice seemed relaxing. The tone. His words. Easing the tension from her shoulders. Lost in thought, almost missing when he told them to put her order on his bill as well.

"You don't have to do that."

"Hopefully it'll make your day better."

"Thank you." Whispered from my lips. Placing my order as he was ready.

Watching as he left. He turned once again and smile. "Hope your day gets better." Pushing through the door, back into the world he went.

"You don't know what you want? That's a first."

"I panicked. What did you want me to say?"

"Oh, I don't know. Hi, can I have my usual. That would have worked."

Niki was laughing at me. Mia and her owned a quaint, rustic coffee shop 'Common Grounds'. It had been home since her mother passed away. Walking the street hundreds of times before and never noticed the place. Then, one day, it was just there. Calling to her, she'd been hooked ever since.

Feeling transported to another place whenever she entered. Never went with anyone. Just grabbing a coffee and book. Hiding in the back corner, trying to lose herself in another world. The building was an old century brick, almost hidden from sight. Once through the door, a rustic charm took hold. Vaulted ceiling and wood beam accents. The walls were whitewashed wood, a scattered assortment of pictures decorating them.

Wood tables, softened by a mixture of leather chairs and stools. Along the back stood a stone fireplace reaching for the sky. Rounded rocks, carefully placed, each one holding a story of their own. There was always a soft fire glowing inside. Wood benches on either side. Homemade pillows and blankets rested against them. Along the edges were shelves lined with books for sale, or simply to read while you enjoyed a drink.

Grabbing the spot, curling up sipping a drink. Those eyes. Ones she'd never forget. Someone had to do something about this soon, or she'd be lost thinking about him for the rest of the day. The

9

warmth of the drink eased her nerves. It didn't matter if it was hot out. Taking away her coffee, something no one would dare to do.

Liquid gold, the velvety taste, the smell of home. All rolled into one giant cup of goodness. Bad day...have a coffee. Cold outside...have a coffee. Flashes of my uncle interrupted her thoughts. The flames captured her gaze, as if protecting her. Glazing at her watch, she was late for meeting Mary. How had so much time passed? The squeak of the chair, distracting my thoughts of his emerald green eyes. Niki's raised eyebrow had other ideas.

"What?"

"Excuse me."

"Sorry Niki, it has been a bad day."

"I can tell, want to talk about it? I've been in your shoes before remember."

"Not really. Thanks."

"I'm here if you need me kid."

"Kid? Really? You're not that much older than me."

"Old enough."

She knew when to question Adrianna and when not to. Today, was a 'not to day'. Watching as she walked back behind the counter, greeting her next customer. As the door closed behind, I knew it wouldn't take long to find Mary. Walking along the street admiring the sights, there usual spot wasn't far away.

The entrance to the park was at the end of the path, winding around the lake. An iron bridge with wooden planks was the way over. Fairy Lake if you really wanted to know.

As a kid, her mom would bring her to feed the ducks. Remembering looking through at the trees, wondering if real Fairies lived here. Waiting ever so patiently in hopes one would appear. Afraid to cross the bridge to the park. Each time, making her mom check to make sure there wasn't a troll, waiting to steal her away.

Laughing now at how silly her thoughts were. Brick posts supporting the four corners of the red iron structure. Mary perched on top. Legs swinging with her RBF firmly in place.

"So?"

"So? What?"

"You ignored my texts all day, then send me pic of a coffee cup. What?"

"Now where is the fun in that. Plus, I had a shit day and didn't want to be bugged."

"You seem better now?"

"Let's just say it had some good moments."

"How good of moments?"

Like the air had carried her. Mary effortlessly touched the ground as she jumped from her spot. Not a sound made. Adrianna never understood how someone could move so quietly.

"How did you find that place?"

Grabbing the cup out of Ad's hand, just before she could finish. Coffee spilt down her shirt. Glaring as if Adrianna had done something wrong. Mary stood there waving the cup in her face.

"Really? That was my coffee. What the hell-"

"When did you go there?"

As if she'd suddenly grown a second head, Adrianna stared at her friend. It was a coffee shop. Like she wouldn't find it. Mary knew better, Adrianna's blood was fueled by coffee.

"I've been going there a while. I found it after my mom died. What's your problem anyway?"

"I've got to go."

Mary stormed way. Pitching what was left of the coffee in the trash. There was something wrong. This wasn't how she acted. It's like, Adrianna found a secret hideout or something.

The sun was still high in the sky. Usually, Ad always come with someone here. Now to think of it. She'd always gone with someone. Staring down the path. Its pull, drawing her deeper. The beams of suns light filtered through the trees. Something was different today.

Warm heat surrounding Ad like a blanket. Comforting me. Holding her in place. Each time she wanted to take a step; her feet felt like weights. Holding Ad firmly in place. The haze that had been visible the other day was thicker. Harder to see through. An eeriness held in it. How could the beauty of one day, turn so drastically the next? Staring into the abyss of trees, wondering what secrets it held.

Having been there a thousand times. Why was today different? Why was Mary acting strange? So many questions flooding to her mind. Having come to talk to Mary. She'd left. Abandoned Ad on a day when she needed her. What was up with that? Something reached for her hand. Gently feeling as if being pulled back to reality. Cotton candy colors covered the sky. Shades of orange and pink sat below the now purple clouds. It couldn't be, the sun was just up? Now, it was slipping over the trees in the distance. How long had she been standing there, Adrianna wondered?

"Sorry. I didn't mean to scare you. You were standing there for a while and wanted to make sure you were alright."

It was him again, from the coffee shop earlier. Shaking her head, trying to focus on things around, confused how she'd lost so much time.

"I'm fine. Just lost in thought again I guess."

"I was heading to the café. Would you like to come? It's getting dark, and since you've been here since this morning, I'm going to guess you walked."

"Sure, I could use something to drink. I still don't know where the days have gone."

"It happens to everyone one." A soft smile on his lips, his eyes catching the last rays of light.

It wasn't far. Grateful for the company. The hustle of the day was replaced with the music and laughter of night. It was a warm summer night. The perfect time for patios on Main. Each one was full. People enjoying food and drink while catching up with family and friends. Teenagers waiting at the ice cream store, with the usual line up out the building. The comic book and novelty shop had people wandering in and out. It was the place to be at night. It took on a life of its own.

They were far enough down the street; Adrianna could see Mary and two other girls leaving the shop. What was she doing there? She'd acted all bitchy earlier, then just left. Niki waved through the window. Her expression changed when she'd realized Adrianna was with him again. The door was propped letting the night sounds in. As if on cue, the sounds of crickets and nightlife filled the room.

Grabbing a seat by the window. Not wanting to miss the nightlife. The back was where Adrianna went to be alone. Her escape from reality, that she wasn't ready to share that yet. A round table in front of the window with a full-size screen facing the street. Almost crammed into place. Just enough room to squeeze in. Watching as he got our order. Niki telling him something, low enough that she couldn't hear. They both made their way, joining me. He slipped out the chair, turning to straddle it, while she took the seat across from mine. Silence filled the air. None of us were in a rush to fill it. Smiling into the cup as she raised it to my lips.

"Good?" The one question with multiple meanings. Just which meaning was she searching for?

"Good. Thank you." Winking at her.

There was no pressure to talk. Still afraid to ask his name. She just wanted to live in the moment, and not worry about anything past then. He hadn't asked hers either. He made her feel safe, and had Niki's blessing, that's all that mattered at the moment.

"Thanks for the hot chocolate and tarts. It's getting late. I should get going."

"I'll walk you home."

A soft glow lit the path, old fashioned style light posts. The look transported you back to a different time. Even though they were solar powered now, the look was there. Leaves rustle together, as a small breeze could be felt against her face. The hot weather of earlier, now replaced by a cool summer night. Each step taking them further, away from the smells and noise of restaurants. Replaced by the wildflowers along the path. The sound of the once filled locks, now a slow running creek could be heard. The splash as the ducks and beavers swam threw. Their splashes, the only reminder of life around.

Thankful he walked with her; Adrianna was still shaken from loosing time. Niki, wouldn't have had it any other way. Having must have stopped, he gently squeezed her hand. Adrianna was lost in thought. Staring at her reflection in the water. Like something was looking at her. A section of the path where she used to sit and think. Branches heavy with leave arched over the water. Almost reaching for something to grab. Just inches away. Felt like a metaphor for her life. Close. But, not close enough.

"So. What are we looking at?" Joining me by the edge of the water, he rested against the tree.

"Nothing really. I just kind of like this spot. I seem to stop here all the time."

"Really? Why?"

"Something about it. Like it calls to me. And don't look at me funny either." Not sure why she was telling him. He just made her comfortable.

"Wouldn't dream of it."

Crouching down, leaning closer to the surface. Something moving beneath the surface, not quite seen, but she could feel that it was there. The edge of her foot slowly sank deeper into the wet bank.

As if watching a movie in slow motion, her toes, slightly easing forward. The ground beneath softening, pulling her body with it. Adjusting her feet, trying to stay where she was. Each movement, breaking the ground even more. Reaching for the branch, as the wind shifted, bringing it closer. As if water and wind, were battling for me. One trying to save, the other pulling Adrianna into its dark, murky depths.

Her foot breaking the surface, one still on the ground. Pitching Ad even farther forward. The watery pull on her shoe, adding more weight. Shifting her further. Adrianna could hear the panic in his voice as he tried to reach her. Even being this close, he sounded like he was struggling.

The branch, almost in reach. Struggling to grasp it in her hands. The wind picked up, pushing it even closer, the further forward I went. Seconds felt like minutes. Like each one slower than the last. Fingers grasping, pulling the leaves from the trees. Both hands desperately trying to make contact.

Adrianna's other foot, slipping off the once solid ground, while her legs being pulled deeper into the water. The sturdy branch from the tree now felt beneath my hands. Arching, trying to get a better grip, before the water pulled her in. Locking her hands together. Shoulders aching from the weight of the water on clothes. Watching as he scrambled against the tree. Reaching for me until he had hold of my arm.

"Let go. I got you."

"I can't. I'll fall."

"Look at me. Look at me. I've got you." Panic could be heard in his voice.

His hands tighten around her wrist. Adrianna's gaze going between him and the waters eerie hold. Her eyes, filling with hot fiery tears, while pain searing through her arms. Releasing one hand, as the others grip deepened into the bark. The shrill sound of the leaves, almost like the tree itself called out in pain. His grip tightened. His hold secure.

"Let go. I got you."

The steely sound in his voice, Adrianna needed to concentrate on that. Had to focus on him. Nodding to him. Needing his strength to let go. Breaking her hold, as her body sank deeper into the water. Reaching with her free hand. Stopping the watery descent. The water releasing its hold, while the wind diminished to the soft summer breeze once again. Finding the soft ground beneath her, not stopping until she was far enough away. The solid asphalt of the path felt underneath her touch, while terror held its firm grasp on her mind.

"Hey. It's ok. You're alright. You're safe."

"HOW MUCH MORE ARE YOU GOING TO THROW AT ME!"

Hot tears streaming down her checks. As she screamed the words to the world. Pulling her knees up to her chest, wrapping her arms around them. Cocooning into a ball.

"Hey. It's ok. I'm here. You're safe."

He sat down wrapping his arms around her soaked body. Adrianna let her body sink into him. She'd let someone else be strong for once. His comfort was the only thing she wanted, need right now. The hot dry feeling in her eyes, as there were no more tears left to cry. The back of Ad's hands smeared the water-stained tears on her cheeks. Lungs burning as the air once again filling them. Each breath calming the flames within.

"Thank you, again. You seem to always be bringing me back from the brink."

"Hey. Don't worry about it. I'm just glad you're alright."

"I think I just want to go home. I can walk the rest of the way from here. I'll tell Niki that you took me the whole way. I just need some time to myself."

"Are you sure, I don't mind."

"I'm sure. Thanks again."

Pushing herself off the ground. It was only a few more streets. Wanting only to go home, shower, and go to bed forgetting the day even happened.

CHAPTER TWO

Years had gone by, still Adrianna had no desire to do anything. Living day by day, the only advantage was that she never saw her uncle again after the funeral. After Mary moved away, they still remained close, Ad wished they lived closer so she could visit her more, it had been years of just phone calls. Video call was great, but still wasn't the same as seeing your only friend face to face.

Lying, staring at the ceiling Adrianna wondered what life would have been like if her mother was still alive. How different would her life have been; wishing only for the nightmares to stop. The day her mother died was the first one she'd ever had, and they came more frequently as the years went on. It was the same dream every time, she'd awake before it finished. It was one dream she wanted to know the ending of.

Being taken somewhere; hidden from someone she cared about. Her abductor was always just an outline, never making out the features. The person radiated pure evil, she could feel it with every fiber of her being, but deep down she knew who the person was. Knowing that they shared something, but unsure what.

Her prison was a room with no exits, but bright, she could see everything. Someone didn't want her found. Pictures lined the walls; they almost seemed alive as the images in the moved about. Each time a feeling of dread washed over her, and she'd wake up. Never knowing if she'd be rescued or not. Secretly wishing for someone to find her, and save her.

Just once though, Adrianna wanted to know the ending, wanting closure of the dreams. Mentioning it to Mary a few times. Her friend kept putting it off as a vivid imagination. By the look in her friend's eyes, Adrianna felt that Mary was holding something back. She just hoped that one day the dreams would stop.

Brushing off the night before, trying to make the most of her day off, even she knew that spending too much time in her own imagination was never a good thing. Sitting on the couch in her comfy clothes and watching re-runs on the TV sounded great to her. Hearing the door bell, not being in the mood for salesman she ignored it. Unfortunately, whoever kept ringing it had other ideas.

Dragging herself off the couch, body still sleepy from the night before; opening the door to see a man standing there. He was wearing a designer suit, guessing it cost more than her monthly pay. As he cleared his throat, she realized she must have been staring longer than she thought. Emerald eyes met her at the door. Dark polished hair, with each strand neatly tucked into place. Tailored suit hugged his frame, the collar accentuating his sharp jaw line, while a crisp tie laid against his chest.

"Um, Hello, Can I help you?"

"Are you Miss Adrianna Lucia Macilli?"

"Yes, may I ask who you are, and why you're at my door?"

"My name is Luc Vero and I'm an attorney sent from the law firm your father deals with." Staring at the woman in front of him. He'd met her before, unable to remember where. Luc knew there was no doubt who her family was. She was beautiful with her messy hair and no make-up. He could already see the family resemblance.

"I'm sorry? I don't have a father, or at least not one that I ever met."

"May I come in and I will explain everything? Apparently, there is a lot to know."

"I already know everything I need to about him, sorry not interested."

"Really Miss Macilli, I think you'll be interested in what I have to say." Not willing to give up that easily yet, he waited patiently for an answer.

"Fine, come in." Turning and catching a glance of herself in the mirror, the look of horror on her face. Her hair wasn't even brushed, face still tired looking from the night before; not the way she wanted to meet a man, especially one that looked like him.

Showing him the family room and offering him a seat, she couldn't wait to hear what he had to say. As far as she was concerned, she didn't have a father. Sperm donor yes, but it took more than that to be a dad. He left her mother alone and pregnant, any man that would do that, Adrianna didn't have a use for.

"Sir, I don't know what you think you have to say, but trust me; I already know everything that I want or need to know about my so-called father." Bitterness dripping off her voice, trying to make her point clear. Whatever he wanted to say she really didn't want to hear. Staring at him, with his dark hair and soft green eyes would make listen to what he had to say more tolerable though.

"Miss Macilli."

"Ad, call me Ad. I'm sure you couldn't have that much to tell, except that my father is a deadbeat." As if trying to protect her heart from being broken again, instinctively crossed her arms over her chest.

"There, you are completely wrong in your judgment of him." Sensing her feistiness, and the spark shining in her eyes. He knew that wording what he had to say properly, was going to be the key.

"Wrong? How can you say I'm wrong? You don't even know me. I've had the last five years to go through it in my mind. Alone, no mother, no father, just me. So, say whatever you have to say quickly, because I'm not in the mood."

"Why don't we start by you telling me exactly what your mother has told you, and then I will fill in the blanks." Seeing how hard she was trying to keep herself together, the sheen in her eyes, the soft pout of her bottom lip, he was going to have to tread slowly.

"What else, I told you. My father left my mother when she was pregnant, his family didn't like her and told him it was either them or her, he chose them. Mom never talked about him other than that. Whatever secrets she had; she took with her when she died. Get it! So really, I don't need some man to come in saying that my father sent him. If he wanted to make sure that I get nothing, I could care less, he gave me nothing growing up, so I don't need it now."

"What do you mean your mother died five years ago? We were never aware of that; we would have found the death record." Something was wrong, questions were growing; not only about Adrianna, but the entire situation as well.

"Would you like me to take you to the cemetery and prove it? Is that what you want?" Even saying the words stung, she hadn't been there in months. It was just too hard each time she went.

"No, I believe you, it's alright. Let's try this again. The reason I am here is that your father never abandoned your mother. He searched for years, with no clues to where she went."

"Really? It couldn't have been that hard, I have been here my whole life."

"In this house? This is where you have always been?"

"Did I stutter."

"Sorry, can I finish."

"Sure, why not."

"Like I was saying, your mother left one day for an appointment, and she never came back. He had the best detectives looking for her but nothing. It was like she disappeared off the face of the earth. All he wanted was to watch you grow up, he wanted to make sure you were taken care of." Reaching in his pocket, pulling out one of the envelopes, she clearly wasn't ready for both.

"So, you're telling me everything my mother told me was a lie. I can't accept that."

"As I told you, he wanted to make sure you were looked after." Handing her the envelope he got up to leave. "If you have any questions, please, feel free to call." Pulling out a business card, placing it on the coffee table, he left.

Sitting there, watching as he walked out the front door after dropping a bombshell at her. Hearing the click of the latch as the door closed, walking over to the window, she put the envelope on the table, watching him pull out of the driveway and down the street. Curiosity getting to her, staring at the manila envelope on the table; she grabbed it heading back to the couch.

Sitting there, wishing that the man who just said her entire life was a lie didn't walk out the door. Shaking her head, contemplating all the different emotions going through her mind at the moment. Thinking that getting her head checked would have be a better option. Staring at the envelope, untying the latch at a turtle's pace out of fear of what the contents might hold. Slipping the papers out, staring in disbelief; there's no way Adrianna thought.

The check she held in her hands had more zeros on it than she could imagine. The address on the bottom of the check was the same bank she used. Sitting there stunned, considering the option that the entire thing was some joke. No one would really do this for a kid they've never meet. Putting the check down Adrianna left it sitting there for weeks. Daily she walked past it, still in shock; not wanting to believe what he said was true. Why would her mother lie to her? What possible reason would some stranger claiming to be her father come into her life now?

Finally, the day came; she needed to know if the check was real or not. Hesitantly handing the teller the check waiting for the 'ha ha this is all a joke moment.' It never did, with a smile the teller deposited the check, and asked if Adrianna needed help with anything else. Her life had just changed. No need to go to her crappy job at the box store anymore. No more worrying about paying rent each month, or how to cover the bills. She had a new life thanks to Mr. Luc Vero; but unfortunately, she had more questions than she did before.

Reaching in her pocket, pulling out the warn business card. Adrianna had held it so many times she knew it by heart. The sleek black card with gold lettering, his name rose off it as if jumping into her hand. How many times she had let her fingers glide over them, caressing each letter as if they burned to be touched. Adrianna chose today for new beginnings, she figured why not go for all or nothing, she didn't have anything else left to lose.

Putting the car in gear, driving to his office to get answers for her questions. The answers wouldn't bring back her mother, or connect her to the father she never knew; but what if he was right? What if her whole life she had it wrong? Maybe her father had spent his life looking for her? He could have been just as lost as she had been the last few years. Getting the answers, she needed would allow her to live the life she'd always dreamt about. Laying the past to rest once and for all.

As a smile crossed her face, hope shining in her eyes; like a candle just lit she was ignited from a flame within. Still afraid of what she might find after, sheltering herself in a cocoon for such a long time. Spreading her wings to be free was her first step, today was as good as any day.

CHAPTER THREE

Staring out the window of his office, watching as the soft flakes fell from the sky silently drifting towards the earth. Each one different, and alike at the same time. Their soft shape and form brought images of Adrianna to mind. She hair pulled back into a messy bun, the icy cold exterior that he knew was heated with warmth underneath. Like a shell protecting her from harm. He couldn't blame her though, not after what she had been through.

That one day, etched in his mind, wreaking havoc on him. There was something about her, the effect she held over him. Luc needed to keep his feeling in check, it was his job. The last thing his boss needed was him lusting after this client. Just the image of her answering the door, all cozy and warm; her sitting on the couch listening as he told his story. Watching as her guard flew up in order to protect herself. He wanted to be the one to protect her; he wanted to be the one she leaned on.

Seeing the reflection in the window as his boss entered the office. He was use too him just popping in. A nod in acknowledgement gave him a second to turn around and focus.

"Hi sir, how was your trip. Hope you're well rested."

"You seem a little sidetracked Luc, everything alright?"

Watching as his boss tried to read the situation. All Luc could do was wait; knowing that he wouldn't like what he was about to tell him. He didn't have much of a choice, he was going to find out one way or another that everything didn't go as planned.

"Everything's fine. I took care of the Miss Macilli situation for you. But there was a little snag."

Waiting for Mr. G's response, Luc could see him contemplating the outcome in his head. He was one man that Luc never wanted to cross. He really had no worries where Mr. G was concerned, but this situation was more delicate than most of the ones they were working on. After meeting Adrianna, Luc was going to make sure that the case file stayed with him, he didn't want anyone else involved in this. She was his, and soon everyone would know it. Protecting her was an instinct he couldn't let go of. No matter what, he'd make sure that no one harmed her ever again.

Drifting back into the recesses of his mind, picturing her dark curly hair, crystal blue eyes, she wasn't short but not tall either, the perfect height, and curves in all the right places. She wasn't a stick like most of the girls were trying to be, she embraced her curves even if she wasn't aware of it. He would be the one she'd run to when something was wrong. Not that Luc would dare saw any of it to his boss. With a roll of his neck bringing himself back to reality, the dreams he would save for later.

"What kind of snag are we talking about? You were to drop off two envelopes and leave, that was it. What went wrong?"

"Well, sir, for starters she didn't know anything about her father. She was told that he abandoned her mother before she was born."

"Her mother said what?" That crazy bitch told her that her father just up and left!" Redness creeping over his face, feeling the heartbeat in his ears; his hands gripping the back of the chair as he launched it into the wall.

Seeing the situation quickly escalating, he needed to regain control before Mr. G lost it even more. He couldn't risk any of this taking place in the building, there would be too many questions if something happened. Luc could only cover up so much. Each time his boss did something it became harder to hide. It was like waiting for a simmering volcano to erupt, which never ended well for those directly in front.

"Ok, sir. Just relax, I'll fill you in on everything. Uncle! I can't tell you if you blow the place up!" Staring at his uncle from across the room, he hoped he could get through to him.

Crossing the room to retrieve the chair, his uncle took his seat behind the desk waiting for Luc to tell him exactly what had happened.

"Alright, her mother lied to her, her entire life about not being wanted; then leaves a teenager by herself at vulnerable age, not knowing her true identity when she passed away. How could she?"

"I wish I had more answers. Adrianna was already in shock at the fact her father had been looking for her for years. I didn't think she could handle the full truth. So I left the envelope with the check, and my business card for her if she had any questions. The bank just notified me that she cashed the check. It took her six weeks; do you really think that I should have pushed it further; I'll go back there right now if you'd like. She needs time to sort things out. Trust me, she'll call when she needs answers."

Silence surrounded the office; Luc knew that his uncle was evaluating everything he had just learned. Just telling his uncle the story he wanted to rush back and coddle Adrianna like a little lost child. He needed to keep his feelings hidden deep down; no one needed to know about them yet.

"Uncle, I left the check, and told her that her father wanted her to be taken care of. That he spent years looking for her. I didn't want to push her anymore; she was in shock. Her mother is dead, and finds out her life was a lie, how would you react?"

"How did you not know her mother was dead? Didn't you check all the records?"

"That's the thing, we did. There's no record of it."

32

"So, when will you tell Adrianna the rest? It can't be hidden for much longer?" Cocking an eyebrow and his nephew they both knew there was more at stake and she would need answers sooner than later. "You better know what you're doing Luc, I'm trusting you with her life on this one. If you screw up your more than just fired, understand."

"Yes sir." Screwing this up wasn't even an option. This woman had already carved out a piece of herself in his life, she just didn't know it yet.

"I'm leaving for a few days. I need to sort a few things out. I need to track down my kids, it been too many years even for them. You know how to reach me. I trusting you with her life DON'T forget that." A sinister look flashed in his uncle's eyes making sure his point came across.

"She'll be my first priority."

Without saying another word his uncle was gone, Luc really hated when he did his whole vanishing act. At least this time he'd come in, and out the same way; so no one would have seen him hopefully. He was going to have to remind him again that humans used the doors and didn't flash from place to place. Either that or get tinted windows installed so no one could see in. Each time he flashed it meant that they were closer to getting caught. Even though most of the people in the building were all similar, the few humans, they employed didn't need to be snooping around.

At least they lived in the age of plastic surgery, Botox, chemical peels and any other medical procedure that could make you look younger. In a society that tried to be ageless they could blend in, but only for so long. You didn't get to be their age without being careful, and people could only believe genetics for so long.

Staring out the window again before starting back to work, he needed to clear his mind. He watched as the red car slipped into the spot out front, as images of her burned into his mind. He would be of no use to his uncle or Adrianna if he couldn't keep his thoughts straight. He was just glad his uncle couldn't read them.

Finding a spot in front of the building, Adrianna slipped her red cougar into it. Turning off the engines, sitting there for a moment to remember why she'd drive there again. Earlier it seemed like a great idea, now that she was here, nerves were beginning to set in. Checking herself in the mirror, it was now or never, if she didn't get out now, she wasn't going to.

Catching a glimpse of her reflection in the car window. Wearing low-rise jeans, t-shirt, hoodie, runner and a baseball cap, wasn't the way she'd want to make a first impression. She wasn't going to change who she was. With her confidence building back up, she would grab the bull by the horns, and go for it.

Walking up the concrete steps, in awe of the view that lay before her; it was as if time stood still. There was no litter; the steps were void of ice and snow; where the rest of the town lay covered in a cashmere blanket of it. Looking up the building that seemed lost in the clouds as it reached for the sky. A smoky colored glass enclosed the entire building, cloaking it so it may disappear into the night. It seemed familiar to Adrianna, like she'd been there before, knowing right where to find everything. Like she was meant to be here, she belonged there.

Entering the lobby walking past the reception, she knew right where to go, the person behind the counter just smiled as she walked by. Absorbing everything that surrounded her, the antique chair in the corner beside a column, the water feature that rested by the wall beside the elevator. As a chill ran down her spin as she stared at her reflection threw its mirror like ambiance with steel behind it. Staring into it, it seemed like it was looking back, she thought.

Almost like they waited for her, the doors to the elevator slowly opened beckoning her into it. Reaching for the top button knowing that's where she would find the offices. Millions of questions flooding to her. This man was the only key Adrianna had to her father. If Mr. Vero could fill in the blanks, at least she would have the answers; after spending years trying to pry from her mother. Electricity was flooding her veins with excitement, her mind reeling, fear and nervousness threatening to consume her at any moment.

Her palms warming at the thoughts, rubbing them on her jeans, hoping the friction would cool them before she reached her destination. Second guessing if she had made the right choice, the closer she came to the floor. Should she have booked an appointment? What if he wasn't even in the office? Adrianna couldn't do this, her stomach tightening with fear the more she thought about it.

With pen bouncing off his desk, Luc turned to stare out the window trying. To focus his energy which was bouncing off the walls at the moment. The historical buildings, trees and paths he could see in the distance. What the hell was he going to do? He needed to see her again, and couldn't wait. With no good reason to go back, she wasn't ready for the other envelope yet. He was obsessing; over a woman he'd met once.

'You can call me Ad' she said to him, he preferred Adrianna, didn't she realize how beautiful her name sounded. There was something more, something he was missing. Maybe seeing her would help in figuring it out he thought. Pushing out of his chair, making his way from the office, just a quick visit.

Not realizing how fast the elevator was she was at the floor in moments. As the doors slid open, she saw him. The whole office had glass walls, so much for just showing up, but the smile on his face she knew that he'd seen her.

Feeling his heart start to pound in his chest, excitement building, she'd come. Tightening in the pit of his stomach thinking something was wrong. Wanting to rush right out there to meet her, restraining himself so he wouldn't scare her away. Buzzing the receptionist telling her to show Miss Macilli in. Drawing a deep breath to calm his nerves; feeling like a boy again.

Making her way to his office, he'd seen her so there was no backing out now she thought. The receptionist waved her in. On the wall beside the door was a brass nameplate, wanting to reach for it to rub her fingers across it, she quickly stopped herself.

Watching her hesitate for a moment, he walked over and opened the door for her. Captivated as she slowly lifted her head to meet his gaze; hoping that he wasn't blushing like a child. Showing her in, Luc offered her a seat as he leaned against the desk.

"Good day Miss Macilli and what brings you by today?"

"I was in the area, and you said that if I had any question I should stop by." Stuttering trying to get the words out, Adrianna silently hoped she didn't sound like an idiot.

"You didn't have any problems with the check, did you?" Knowing full well that she hadn't, the bank notified him as soon as it was cashed. Seeing the unease in her, helping ease the conversation.

"No. Not at all, thank you again. It just took me a while to cash it; the whole thing was just surreal to me."

"It must have been a lot for you to take in. We truly didn't know that you were unaware of the situation."

"Just never came from much, so to have someone say here you go. Giving you a gift that will change your life forever….it took a while to adjust. That's all."

"So, what have you done with your new found wealth?"

"Well, I quit my job today; I've worked there since high-school so it felt good."

Seeing the smile spread across her face, and a spark in her eyes as she spoke, he knew she was happy. Her mouth slightly opened, lips full and inviting, he could stare at her all day. Wanting nothing more than to hold her in his arms. With glass walls this was no place to though, he'd always kept his private life just that, private. He wasn't about to change that now.

"So now with no job and all the money in the world, what are you going to do Adrianna?"

A sly smile spread over her face, questions she'd asked herself her entire life, and now with the means, Adrianna had her answers.

"Take the path less travelled; I'm going left when the rest of the world leans right. It's time for a change. I've spent the last five years trying to keep a roof over my head, going through the motions but not really living. Now, I can do just that. Live, and see what life is truly about for once."

"Your father would be proud of your decision." She was more like him then she'd ever know, with more years left than she could fathom. Luc would make sure she enjoyed every one of them. Her age still confused him, how was she so young when her mother vanished a century ago. Only leaving him with more questions. Or had her memories been wiped to hid her age?

"You say my father would be proud, and that he wanted me to have certain things. Did you know him?" The only tie to her father was sitting in the same room with her, she prayed he'd have the answers she needed.

Luc's heart melted a little as she asked the question. He had all the answers she needed, but he'd have to tell her slowly, there was more at stake than either of them ever would realize. Breaking the news to her would change the world as Adrianna knew it. Anticipation growing, Luc looked forward to discovering more about who she really was.

"I knew your father very well, practically all my life. I would like to tell you everything. It could take a while however; we have a long history."

"I would appreciate that very much; you're the only link I have to a life I never knew existed. I don't know which part is true or a lie anymore there are so many blurred lines."

Rubbing her hands together, it was something she'd always done since a child. It soothed her, and the slow warming made her feel secure, the more they warmed the better she felt.

"The only thing I can tell you for certain Adrianna; is that no matter what happened along the way, both your parents loved you very much."

"Thank you, no one has said that in a long time; sometimes it's just nice to hear. With a smile she tucked a stand of hair behind her ear, knowing that soon all her questions would be answered.

"Why don't we go get a coffee, you can ask me a few questions. We will take it slowly, so you can think about everything you want to know."

"Sure, that would be great."

Silently Adrianna smiled. Water welled in the corners of her eyes, but quickly disappeared. For the first time in a long time, she'd have answers, the company of a handsome man, and a life to look forward to. Luc Vero was her key to the future she could feel it. Rising from the chair watching as he opened the door, following him towards her future.

CHAPTER FOUR

Walking silently down the street towards the coffee shop, giving her the space, she needed. No matter how confident she came off, he could still sense the lost girl inside. He wanted her trust above all else. Watching as the snow once again fell around them, seeing the beauty of it, wondering if she saw it as well. In all his years he never enjoyed it as much as he did today. Absorbing the essence of it completely, taking in every last sight. They were all so beautiful, seeing the variations with each one as it floated by.

Enjoying the walk, Adrianna thought about all the questions she wanted to ask, with no idea where to begin. Walking beside him gave her a sense of safety, a feeling she'd never felt before, something she craved now more than ever. Smiling to herself she knew that destiny had brought them together, to this place. For whatever reason, this was where she was supposed to be right then and there. Catching his reflection passing by the store window she wondered what was going through his mind at the moment. He was deep in thought she could tell.

Opening the door to the store, the smells overwhelmed her. The scents of hot chocolate, vanilla, teas and coffee came floating to her through the air. Gingerbread, apple cider, encircling her. Never had she experienced it before, it soothed her making her happier.

"What can I get you?"

Pausing for a moment while memories flooded back to her. The scents of the coffee, those eyes. It was him. The boy who'd helped her all those years ago. Did he remember it was her all this time? Did he even remember who she was? How was he back in her life once again?

"An extra-large apple cider please, thanks you. Please let me."

"It's alright Adrianna, you can get the next one."

"Thank you. You don't remember me, do you? I finally know why you seem so familiar." Feeling a flush creep over her cheeks, and butterflies in her stomach she smiled. It was like when she was with him, she didn't know who she was anymore. Like the lost piece of her that had been missing was found again.

"The coffee shop? That was a lifetime ago." Luc now flooded with memories of that day, if he would have only known. What blinded his visions of her that day.

"That was right after my mother had died. Sorry I never knew your name back then. There was just so much going on, I wasn't in the best place."

"That's alright. Don't worry."

Luc had all the answers she was searching for, every detail about a father she never knew. Anticipation and fear growing at the same time; he could see it in her eyes. He didn't want to rush, wanting as much time as he could spend with her.

"Adrianna, why don't you tell me about your life with your mom, that way I can fill in the blanks. I'd really like to know what happened."

Staring at the whipped cream slowly melting from the warmth of the cider, she contemplated where to begin. Avoiding the past had gotten her to where she was today. Blocking it out for so long was her way of coping. With a lump growing in her throat, she'd have to unlock the part of her she kept hidden from the world. It was the only way Adrianna would be able to get the answers she desperately needed.

Watching as the sheen glossed over her eyes, she slid them shut in silence as if battling demons from within. Shoulders rising then slowing easing back down, centering herself, he could see the tension leaving her body. As she peered from beneath her hat, her eyes glowed; he knew that she was ready.

Starting at the beginning she retold the story; as her mother had told her each time she asked about her father when she was a child. All Adrianna wanted was a complete family growing up, and it was the one thing she never received. Telling Luc how her father left before she was born. That his family never liked her mother, felt that she was beneath them yet they had never meet her.

Her mother said the only way he would introduce them was after they were married, but mom didn't want to get married just because she was pregnant, that it was for the wrong reason. The last time her father had asked, her mother said no. So her father told Nina to go have the baby herself then and left.

Seeing the emotion etched in the words as she spoke them. Luc knew how hard it must have been for Adrianna to tell him the story. He wanted nothing more than to comfort her; fighting his own inner turmoil not to rush over and scoop her up in his arms. With each addition to her past, his gut clenched at the thought of what her life must have been like. Having no idea of the truth, of how much her father loved her mother, and would have done anything for them.

Learning that they lived where he found her since birth shocked him. That her and her father were so close to each other, and so far at the same time. How the neighbor helped raise her as if her own grandchild so that Nina could work to support them. Once the neighbor had passed away it was only Adrianna and her mother. Luc knew that he would have to watch his words telling her. Pain ran deep, and he didn't want to tarnish the image of the only parent she'd ever know.

He was grateful she had her friend Mary for support through the funeral, and the years that followed. Her uncle sounded like a first-class jerk and was glad he was out of her life. Watching as the sun slowly sank behind the buildings, realizing they had been gone for hours. Luc had yet to tell her anything about her father's family.

Adrianna amazed him, with everything she'd been through, she still felt hope. She had no idea of the life she could have had if her mother never ran away. How her father would have done anything for them. Watching as she shifted uneasily in her seat.

"I'm sorry that I took up your day. You should have stopped me, I'm sure you were busy."

"No, it's fine really. I had an amazing day listening to your story." Deep down Luc didn't want their time to end, the day had gone by so quickly.

"If felt good talking to someone, it's been such a long time since I've talked about my mom. Talking helps me remember her."

"I'm glad, it helps me understand you better. I knew your story would be very different from the one I know. I assume you already knew that though."

"The funny thing is, I don't even know what my father looked like. Mom never had any pictures of him. He was just some faceless man in my imagination. I'd walk down the street and look into men's faces when I was little hoping I'd see something. A feature of my own, and I'd know it was him. But that was just wishful thinking of a child."

Never dawning on Luc that she didn't even know what her father looks like, he should have said something sooner, put her mind at ease.

"You look a lot like your father. You have his dark hair and blue eye. You get your gracefulness from your mother though. You're a good mixture of them both."

Feeling warm tears beginning to form, no one had ever said that to her before. Her mother always avoided the subject. When she asked what he looked like, so she never knew if she looked like him. Taking a deep breath, she forced back the tears before they could spill, trying to regain her composure.

"Thank you, Mr. Vero, I should get going, it's getting late." Staring at the man before her, not wanting to leave. Emotionally the hours had taken away her energy.

"Wait." Reaching for her hand as she rose from the chair; he wasn't willing to let her go just yet. "Have dinner with me tonight, then I can tell you about your father."

"I'm not sure, it's been a long day...."

"I can tell you about your father. We don't have to go out, I can get take out and bring it to your place. That way you can relax as I tell you everything." Searching her eyes for an answer, feeling the pull they had towards one another slowly burning through them.

"I'm not sure? I was just planning a comfortable evening in, track pants and t-shirt type of thing…."

"Sounds good to me; if you are up to it." Comfy clothes sounded good, deep down he was picturing her wearing a little less. If his boss ever found out his feelings for her, there would-be hell to pay. Watching as she bit her bottom lip. He was going to be in more trouble than he thought if she kept that up.

"Sure, um, alright, we can order take-out or something."

"You go home and relax, I'll pick up something on my way, I'll be there about seven, is that alright?"

"Sure, see you then." Confused on how going home alone, turned into him bringing dinner, images of how her house look flooded to her.

Walking Adrianna back to her car and saying goodbye, Luc watched as she drove down the street. Smiling to himself, he had two hours to get ready and pick-up dinner. Tonight, was going to be a good night, if he could keep from being tempted.

Pulling into her driveway still in shock, Luc was coming to her house for dinner. Unable to remembering the last time someone had been there. There was the odd guy in school, but since her mom died the only person who use to come was Mary. Since she moved there been no one.

Walking in the door, realization hit her about what a disaster the place really was. There were things everywhere; she'd survived on cereal and take out for so long; she wasn't even sure there was food in the house. Finding some wine in a cupboard and cheese in the fridge it would have to do. Quickly loading the dishwasher and cleaning the counters, making the kitchen look useable again.

Walking down the hall seeing the rest of the house, it looked just as bad she didn't have a lot of time. Attacking the other rooms in the house until they looked presentable, picking up empty chip bags, pop bottles, and used tissues. She hoped that it hadn't looked the same way the last time he was there. By the time she was done, Adrianna thought everything looked presentable enough, she even had time to grab a shower and freshen up.

Glancing at the clock, she still had thirty minutes until he would arrive. Turning on the tap, letting the water warm. Slowly stepping into the shower, while images of Luc came to life. Her body heating at the thought, feeling a blush rise across her heated skin. The water slowly caressed her body. The spray starting at her head, flowing down the length of her. She though of him. It had been so long since she'd craved the touch of others. It consumed her thoughts.

Running the soap along her body, her breasts hardening, nipples gain sensitivity against her touch. Each simple movement sent shivers down her spine, wanting it to be Luc's hand grazing over her body. The warmth of her core drawing her forward, hesitatingly slipping her hand between her thighs. Seeking out the velvety warmth surrounding her fingers. Slowly she slid them in and out, answering the call of her own sex. Her body craving release. Knowing she needed it, craved it. While the flames inside her were building, her pulse accelerating with anticipation. She could hear the phone ringing over the music. Cursing, while her hand slipped from her hot core. Wrapping a towel around her running for the phone, hoping it wasn't Luc cancelling.

"Hello."

"Hello, Miss Macilli, this is Sam from Extreme Window and Doors…."

"You've got to be kidding me; I jumped out of the shower for this! Take me off your calling list! And don't ever call back!"

Slamming the receiver, cursing all the way back to her room; only ten minutes until he'd be there and she still wasn't ready; she'd have to wait till later to finish what she started. Quickly combing out her hair, it was one of the few times she was glad it was curly. Content with how she looked, black leggings, a cream-colored sweater; but just the thought of him coming over had her hormones raging, like a fire consuming a forest with no end.

After watching Adrianna get into her car and drive off, reaching in his pocket placed a call to his favorite Italian restaurant. Ordering prosciutto with melon and seafood antipasto, some pasta alforno, veal in marsala sauce, and cheese cake for dessert and a bottle of Chianti. Hoping it would be a dinner she wouldn't soon forget. Stopping by the florist to grab some daisies, something pretty but not over the top, simple and elegant at the same time.

Going home to change into something less stuffy, he was glad his penthouse was across the street for the law office. Not that anyone he worked with knew, he chose to keep his business life and personal life separate. Tonight, he wanted to be himself, not the lawyer she saw him as. Relaxed and easy to talk with, not an uptight stiff suit. Throwing on a pair of khakis and blue sweater, he couldn't stop thinking of her. Wanting her more than just a client from the first time he laid eyes on her. Thinking back to the first time they'd met all those years ago. Luc wanted to protect her, wanted her to need him as badly as he did her. The feelings were strong even back then. Whatever spell she was using on him was working, even if she didn't know what she was doing yet.

Looking at his watch he needed to get going, he didn't want to keep her waiting for too long. The anticipation was killing him.

Tonight, she'd get to know who he really was, he just hoped that the feeling would be mutual.

Being so involved in the night ahead, he didn't notice the car that had been following
as he left the house. The driver was making sure that the car was far enough behind as to not
to draw any attention. By the way things were going, the driver felt certain that the car was
going undetected. Which was just the way, it was supposed to be.

Exiting the highway, taking the turn so he would go onto Adrianna street; he had this
strange feeling. Just nerves he told himself anticipating the evening ahead. It had been a long
time since he'd been around a woman he was attracted too; it was more than that. He was drawn to her as if Fate herself was pushing them together.

Sitting there, nervous energy humming through her veins, feeling like a kid again anxiously waiting for the doorbell to ring. Hearing the bell her insides heated up with anticipation. Reaching for the handle hesitantly, taking a deep breath to steady her nerves, not knowing where the night would take them but hoping she'd get the answers she had longed for.
Standing there with take out in one hand, a bottle of wine stuffed under

his arm and a bouquet of flowers; she could feel a rush of heat coloring her cheeks.

"Oh, sorry, where are my manners? Won't you come in, let me help you."

"No problem at all, these are for you" he said handing her the flowers and then the wine. "I picked up dinner as well, I hope you like Italian."

"That sounds wonderful, but really you didn't have to go through so much trouble…"

"No trouble at all." Luc said taking in the sight of her looking so at ease in her own home. Thinking back to the last time he was there, shocking her with new she had never expected, he just hoped that this night went a lot smoother.

Following her to the kitchen, breathing in the scents of freshness in the air, reminding him of the home where he grew up. It smelled like springtime in the middle of winter, crisp, clean soft smells filling the space around him. The scent of the daisies he brought her enhancing the illusion he was building in his head. Rolling his neck bringing him back to reality, out of the dream life he once had before everything went wrong.

Watching as she unpacked dinner, opening the bottle of wine he could tell that she was thinking about something. Giving her a few moments until the look of sadness eased off her face. Luc didn't want to push her to fast, but knew that something was bothering her. Opening the bottle of wine, he handed her a glass as a soft smile curved the corner of her lips.

"Is everything alright? If this is too much, we can always do it another time Adrianna."

"No, I'm fine. Was just thinking. It's been a while since I ate anything that remotely looked like a meal, and wasn't out of a box, a can or a frozen dinner."

If she would let him be part of her life, Luc vowed to teach her how to enjoy every moment of her it. Enjoying the wine and meal together, letting small talk lead the way. Never discussing anything important but just letting the conversation flow naturally.

"Dessert looks great, but I really don't have any room right now."

"I'd have to agree. Why don't we go into the other room and relax?" Refilling the glasses, Luc followed her to the family room taking a seat on the couch beside her.

"I'm guessing you have more questions now than you did when you came to the office earlier. Would you like the short or the extended version of your father's life? Trust me when I say the extended is quite long."

"If we're going to do this, you should tell me everything. Please don't feel like you should leave something out. I never knew the man you are going to tell me about, so the more you could tell me the better it is." Jumping in with both feet was the only way she was going to be able to do the Adrianna thought; she just hoped that there were no sharks in the water that would bite back.

Sitting there waiting, parked at the house across the street, knowing that she hadn't been seen. Having all night to sit there, and wasn't about to go anywhere. With a clear view of the house, watching as the bitch became cozy on the couch beside him. Years had been invested in him. She'd be damned if she'd let some woman move in. Making dinner plans with her wasn't the smartest move he'd made. What business could he have with her over dinner that couldn't wait till the morning?

It was all planned out until that dark haired, blue-eyed tramp moved into her territory. Years down the tubes for what? To get shafted; not if she could do anything about it, and she would do something about it! Feeling her anger mounting, rage threatening to take over control. Seeing him turn to face the window, she hadn't come this far to be caught now. Putting the car in gear to leave knowing that they'd meet again, she would be sure of that.

Nearly ripping the door off its hinges as she slammed it shut, did he not realize who he was dealing with? Who was that woman with him? Didn't he realize everything she had done for them to be together? He was hers and she wasn't going to stop at anything to get him back. Anything! That two-bit little tramp wasn't going to get him. Not if she had her way. She always had her way.

Taking pride in her hidden little world, not even her family knew of her home's existence. The secrets that hung in the balance, if anyone were to find them, they would be her undoing. Her trophies brought strength and power with them; if found there would be no question of the chaos that would be unleashed. She was special, the world just had no idea.

Almost being discovered once by her brother, but she had taken care of him, never having any control when he was near her, his anger always getting the best of him. Smirking to herself hoping that he was enjoy the show from where he was. Tormenting him with the people he loved most, while he sat by and could do nothing but watch. He was lucky that was all she had done, but she had been in a good mood that day.

Now she had another problem to deal with, everything was fine until 'she' came along. She wouldn't last long, they never did. All the years she spent planning, only to have some woman come into play now. She'd have Luc for her own, and destroy her father at the same time.

Having the one thing in the world her father held closet to his heart, taking a trophy of the shelf admiring it. It had taken years, but with the help of a friend she finally possessed it. No matter how hard he searched he would never find his one prize. Slamming it back on the shelf the room vibrated with the energy around her. Her trophies swaying in the process, there were many at one time, now there were only a few.

Staring back at his sister from his prison, unable to help anyone. He hoped that whoever her next target is would be strong enough to deal with her. Fate and Destiny had their own plans for his sister, and was definitely wasn't on either of their good sides.

AWAKEN THE FLAMES

CHAPTER FIVE

Glancing out the window, a feeling of unease came over him. Thinking he was wrong but that usually didn't happen, not where he was concerned. If he was being spied on, whoever it was couldn't stay hidden forever. Looking back to Adrianna, curiosity shining in her eyes. Luc knew that she was waiting for him to start, knowing that the story would change her forever; he would choose his words carefully.

Watching as he swirling the contents of his glass around, staring into as if searching for answers Adrianna's anticipation heightened. As he drew in a breath, his shirt tightening across his chest; she hoped he'd start before her mind drifted into a world of its own. As his mouth slightly opened Adrianna hungered for the words she longed to hear, the story of her father, one no one had ever shared. The man of mystery she had built up, and torn down more times than she could count. Sitting before her was the key to the story. She just had to be willing to go through the door once it was opened.

Reaching for her hand, Luc gave it a squeeze before he began, feeling the warmth radiating from her, easing him to start. Staring at the soft pout of her lips and the spark ignited in her eyes he began. Luc explained how her father and his were friends from when they were children; they did everything together from terrorizing girls, causing trouble and bailing each other out. Considered themselves brothers, and the only family either of them needed since their parents weren't around much to help.

As they grew, they started their first business together, a construction company. Putting their heart and soul into everything they built, it wasn't long until they were the biggest company around. My dad met my mom, and seeing how happy they were, my mom introduced him to her cousin who was beautiful and talented. Who turned out to be an underhanded bitch as they learned over the years. She lured your father into a trap and became pregnant a few months after they were together.

"Wait! You're telling me my father was married before, and had a child?" More questions were now surfacing than Adrianna thought possible.

"No, he was never married. Your father couldn't see himself married to a woman who'd trick him into becoming pregnant. That wasn't what your father ever wanted. I know you'll have lots of question. Please let me finish then I will answer all of them." Knowing what must be going through her mind, Luc needed to finish and hoped she would understand when he was done.

As he watched the tension release from her shoulders as she took a sip of the wine, Luc began where he left off. With a sense of duty to his child he stayed with her. Months later she gave birth to a son Sebastian who was your father's pride and joy. He did everything with him, and was determined to protect him from his mother's viciousness. As the years went by, she took advantage of your father again, and became pregnant a second time, this time she gave birth to a baby girl Serina.

Your father spoiled his children with everything they wanted, but your sister was exactly like her mother and manipulated every situation. With their mother only wanting to be with your father forever, and him not wanting the same, Serina became more vicious as the years went on.

Eventually my mother became pregnant with me, but because the pregnancy almost killed my mother, they didn't have any other children because he didn't want to leave me without a mother. Seeing the love my parents had for one another only made their mother anger and jealous. She tried to ruin our father's friendship to no avail, it upset her more that your father promised to raise me if anything ever happened to my parents.

As the years went by their mother became ill, she begged your father to marry her, but he still refused. With all the lives she kept trying to destroy, he felt Destiny would make her own path for her.

"You know the further into the story you go, the more I believe my mom's version of my dad. He wouldn't marry the mother of his children the first time, why would he suddenly want to marry my mom the second time he got someone pregnant?"

"Adrianna, I know your frustration, but please let me finish, it will all make sense in the end." He watched as she took another sip of her wine, sliding closer on the couch, not knowing if she was aware of herself doing it. A smile crossed his face as she was clearly becoming more comfortable with him.

Looking into in her blue eyes, he could tell she was trying to control her emotions while they were burning to be free. Watching as she slowly lowered her lashes for a moment, as they slid open, the fires were gone. Only the shining crystal depths stared back waiting for more answers. Adjusting his position, letting the stress roll up his spine and off his shoulders he continued. As their mother slowly vanished from this world; Serina never forgave her father for what he did. She didn't let her grudge show, she masked it spending much of her time watching me.

My parents had left me with Uncle Sal when they went on a business trip and never returned. Since then, he raised me with Serina's help. Realizing by the look on her face, Luc couldn't believe what he had just did. This entire time he forgot to tell Adrianna her father's name. Seeing the realization across her face, Uncle Sal's name had made everything more real to her in a matter of seconds. How could he have been so stupid he thought?

"Adrianna, I'm so sorry. Your father's name, I forgot."

"It's alright, I've waited years to just know his name and now I know." She managed to say holding back the tears that were threatening to fall. Slowly tilting her head down, she started to weep.

Leaning forward, brushing back a curl from her cheek, watching as her innocence overtook her. No matter how high she built the walls around her heart to protect her, he watched as they slowly crumbled. Moving closer to her on the couch, he wrapped his arms around her offering the comfort she needed.

Letting Luc comfort her, felt right. He infused her with the warmth and strength she needed to continue with the story. Excusing herself for a moment, making her way to the bathroom, splashing cool water on her face to regain composure. Staring at her refection in the mirror. Her eyes flickered like crystals beside a flame, as if a light was shining through a prism. Never noticing before the soft glow of red in the center. As if a small fire had been lite. Left to simmer. Her crystal blue eyes being the hottest part of the flame leading to the red outline at the end, only backwards she thought.

Admiring Adrianna approaching the couch again, she was stronger than most people would give her credit for. Watching as she picked up the bottle of wine and refilled the glasses, handing Luc his giving the cue for him to continue.

With me moving in, Serina had a sudden change of heart towards your father, she helped him with me. Offered to baby sit when he was at work; was the older sibling that I had always wanted. Then one day, she picked up and left without a word. Years went by and then Sal met your mother. She was a breath of fresh air, always smiling and singing, from the minute I met her I knew that her and Uncle Sal would be together forever.

"Alright, hang on, I'm confused."

"About what?"

"If Sal had two older kids that could just leave and not return with no question as to where they went; exactly how much older was my father than my mother?"

"Let's just say it was a few years, not that much by today's standards. But you have to remember he had your sister and brother when he was quite young." Choosing his words carefully, not wanting to reveal too much too soon.

With your mother in his life, your father was much happier. Uncle Sal had asked her to marry him over and over again. Once she became pregnant with you, they chose to keep it to themselves, and not have either Serina or Sebastian find out until your mother agreed to marry him. One day your mom went for an appointment and never came back. Sal was worried sick, he looked for years. Hiring the best investigators money could buy. There was never any trace of either of you. He never knew if he had a son or daughter, you both had vanished and no one ever heard from her again.

62

In all my years I had never seen him as lost as he had been. He searched relentlessly for her. I made him a promise that I wouldn't give up looking until I found you. Then one day there you were, appearing out of thin air, that's the day I came and found you.

"What led you here after all those years?"

"Someone spotted you. Your resemblance to your father was unbelievable, they snapped a photo, we crossed referenced a picture of both your parents. There were too many similarities to be ignored."

Finally having the answers, she longed for, only leaving her with more questions, but with Luc filling in the details and answers for her, she knew the journey would be worth it. Leaning across the couch, giving Luc a hug, he was the link to her past and future, and knew that he'd be there for her. Feeling his strong, muscular arms wrap around her body, infusing her with the strength she needed. He wasn't going to give up until he found her. Now that he found her, she wasn't will to let him go. In his arms was where she wanted to be, with the energy that surged between them, deep down Adrianna knew that he felt the same way.

Holding her there in his arms, Luc couldn't think of a better place to be. It was like they had always been together; they should always be together. Hoping that one day, she'd return the same feelings. Knowing that he had found the one that he could share his life with, and be happy, like his parents.

He should let go, but couldn't. Just wanting to hold onto her for another minute, not pushing his luck, needing her to feel comfortable and not invade too much personal space. Leaning back, placing a soft kiss on her forehead, he hoped she feel better, wishing that he could do so much more.

Feeling the warmth of his hug and the soft kiss on her head, Adrianna looked up and could see that Luc cared about how she felt. All she could feel was energy. It radiating threw her body, like an infusion of heat. Debating what to do and getting lost in the moment; she leaned up and faintly placed a kiss upon his lips. Wanting more, but not wanting to read too much into what she was feeling.

Surprised by the kiss, Luc deepened it. Gingerly leaning in a little more, he slowly and subtly eased his mouth to see if she would follow. He could feel her brush her lips across his, as if wanting and looking for something else. Gathering her up in his arm Luc leaned her back against the cushions, their bodies molding, his into the elegant curves of hers. Designed to fit perfectly together; the gently teasing and blazing hunger of anticipation, consuming them both.

She slid her hand down the sides of his body, savoring each inch. Resting them on his hips while she lifted to meet them. His hand cradled her neck, while he softly left a trail from his lips. Feeling his erection against her center, grinding to get closer. Pulling his sweater up, sliding her hands along his hardened chest.

Aching for her touch, something he'd craved when he met her all those years ago. Not knowing who she was, he would never have let her go. Letting her lead, he didn't want to rush her. Wanting nothing more than to be buried deep inside. Carefully removing her clothes, enjoying each moment as she helped pull the layers away. Every inch of her body would be his to consume. The sly smile curving his lips, letting his excitement show. Sliding on top of her, easing between her legs, his fingers sought out her wet velvety core. Arching her body to meet his demand, seeking his touch like a flame following the fuel.

The warm heat of his mouth moving over her skin, pushing her harder. Nothing had ever felt so good. Her body hummed while the flames seared her veins, stoking the fire buried deep inside. Pulling away, liftin her, he carried her to the bed. Wanting to make it special. Placing her on the floor, standing before her admiring all that she was offering him. He'd been raked with visions of her for weeks, now they would be fulfilled.

Softly while she stood, kissing the curve of her neck, as her head rolled at the sensation, sinking against his touch. His hands slipping lower down her body, his lips following their descent. Pulling her nipples into his mouth, rolling the hard bead against his tongue. All the while her hands gently pulling his hair. Lowering himself to his knees, dragging his tongue along her heated flesh. Nipping at her hips while holding them firmly in his grasp. Looking up, seeing the hunger in her eyes, once again a wicked smile crossed his face.

Lifting her off the floor, resting her against the mound of pillow on the bed. Pulling him against her as she felt the firm mattress beneath. Gliding his hand down her stomach, feeling how wet she was for him. Rubbing her with the palm of his hand while he drove his fingers in and out, until her breathing became like music. Easing back down her body, she knew what was coming next, her breath hitched in the throat.

Teasing her with his mouth, his tongue dipping in and out of her core. The velvety wetness begging him for more. Suckling her center, while his fingers continued their torment. Hi tongue thrusting harder and faster, again and again, feeling the spasms as they ripped through her body. Releasing hold, sliding his body up hers, his erection wanting attention. Pulsing while it slipped into the heat. Their hearts racing with each thrust. Never had he wanted anything as badly as he had right then.

Watching as her head swung from side to side, while waves of pleasure washed over her body. Seeming to glow with electricity that filled the air. The hardened clench before her final climax ripped through her body, joining him. While they laid in each-other's arms, their breathing returning to normal once again. There was no going back to life before, this was their new beginning. Losing themselves until they drifted asleep.

Laying there, holding her sleeping in his arms, he couldn't be happier. She slept so soundly, her breath even and steady. Brushing a curl off her cheek, he could lay there all day admiring her. The flush of color that covered her cheeks, the soft pink of her swollen lips. The candles lit around the room making her body glisten in their light. As if fire danced over her body, the ebony color of her hair radiating as if hot coals in a burning fire. Knowing that she had already changed, he needed to tell her. She would soon figure it out. It had already been at years; hadn't she notice that she wasn't looking any older? How had her mother hidden her the last century? What spell was at work?

He would tell her, but she needed to know a few things about her family first, especially, her sister. If Serina ever knew about Adrianna, there would be trouble, and Adrianna didn't need the likes of her in her life. Grief was one thing Serina had invented, it didn't matter if she was like a sister to him or not. She was a manipulative bitch and would one day get what she deserves.

"Hey can I get you something from the kitchen," he asked as he felt her stir beside him as she snuggled closer to him.

"Mmmm, I would love a glass of water, but I will get it, can I get you anything?" With a lazy smile on her face, she bent her head towards his and captured his mouth.

Watching as she left the room, he knew he had to keep her safe, and knew of only one way how too. He just hoped that she wouldn't be mad at him after when she finds out. But whatever she decides later, he will let her because he was already in love with her. Following her into the other room, she didn't have chance before she could feel his presence behind her. Taking the plate from her, pulling her into his arms, lifting her up with the need to consume her once again.

"The food can wait, I'm suddenly hungry for something else."

His voice laden with sex, crushing his mouth against hers with a desperate need, which she matched on every level. Wrapping her legs around his hips, drawing her closer to her, knowing that he wouldn't break contact. Running the pad of his thumb across the lower edge of her lips. He watched as she nipped his thumb, the feisty fires from the night before still smoldering inside.

"Adrianna, I know that we haven't known each other for very long, but will you stay with me forever, be my forever?"

An invitation had never sounded so nice. Leaning up to brush her lips against his and burning inside with need. She closed the space so that her lips were beside his ears breathlessly whispering to him 'yes'.

Feeling infused with warmth, as if an eruption took place deep within his soul, he loved the idea that he could always keep her safe. No one could harm her without him knowing exactly where she was. Pledging forever to the one you loved, was no different than saying your vows in a church. They would always be bound together. He just hoped that she wouldn't be mad when she found out. Because when you were his age, and you waited this long for the one you wanted; you knew you weren't going to let them go.

AWAKEN THE FLAMES

CHAPTER SIX

Mary hadn't heard from Ad in few days, which wasn't like her, there were always emails, test messages or something between them to stay in contact. Ad never knew that Mary had moved in beside her to protect her. She had to make sure no one found out who she was. Especially Adrianna's sister. There were so many things that Ad didn't understand. When Mary had first met her mother at the clinic, she looked different. When Adrianna was born, she knew right there she was someone special who Mary would fight to protect.

Following them back to where they use to live, Mary changed her hair color, invested in some glasses, and bought the house next door so she could watch them.

Having to move away six years ago was hard, but Adrianna was starting to ask question. One was how well Mary was aging. Mary chose to leave to keep her from knowing the truth until she had too. The whole time though she was never far away. She was able to check in every night while Ad slept, making sure she went very late, so Ad wouldn't notice.

Quickly checking the time, she knew that now was good. It was 4:30am, knowing Ad would be sound asleep. Mary appeared in the blink of an eye, but never expecting to see what was going to in the kitchen, her friend in the arms of a man.

Disappearing before she was seen, she paced around her condo. Funny that Ad had never mentioned a boyfriend the last time that they talked. It hadn't been that long had it? She popped in every night and never noticed anything before. Maybe she should pass by for a visit tomorrow so that they could catch-up. Maybe it was time for her to tell Adrianna the truth, even Mary was still trying to figure some of it out herself, she even had questions as to how Adrianna ended up outside their world.

Luc senses were alive for the first time, even more so his intuition. While they were enjoying being of each other, he felt that there was a presence in the room., but it had vanished as quick, as it had come. Maybe it was just his hyper awareness when it came to her? They were one and the same; and he had never felt anything like it before. He was probably over thinking the whole situation. When he heard the phone ring, he picked up the cordless and went to hand it to Adrianna. It was seven in the morning. There would only be one person calling her this early.

"The phone is ringing would you like to answer it."

"Yea, thanks pass it over. Hello......Oh hi, how are you? Really? Ok, I will see you shortly. Yea; can't wait.... See you soon.... Bye. Sorry, that was my friend Mary I was telling you about, she is in the area and is stopping by. I hope you don't mind the intrusion, she basically is my only friend, besides you of course." She smiled coyly at him as she passed back the phone

"Not a problem, I should really go to the office anyway and check in. How about I leave you and Mary to visit, and come back later this afternoon?" to leave her. For him, finding Adrianna was like a new lease on life.

"You don't have to go. I would love you to meet one another. Promise that you won't be gone long. I really don't want you to go." She said with a sly smile.

Kissing Luc goodbye as he left, fighting the urge to keep him with her, having these feeling of possession generating from her like nothing she'd ever felt before. Deep down hoping she would not be one of those possessive girlfriend types. Getting ready after he left, she couldn't remember the last time she saw Mary, had the last few weeks really been that busy that they hadn't even talked.

Startled by the sound of the bell, taking a deep breath, realizing she was a different person since the last time she'd seen her friend. Opening the door, she let Mary into her new world. It had been six years since they had last seen each other and Mary still looked amazing. Leaning in to give her old friend a hug, she couldn't wait to tell her everything. Their last several conversations were truly about nothing. Ad never told Mary about what her father had left her. Or that she was even thinking about quitting her job.

"O.M.G! Mary it has been so long, I have missed you." Throwing her arms around her friend, Adrianna gave her a long overdue hug.

Feeling like a teenager again, she was happy to see her friend.

"You too Ad, how are things with you?" Thrown by Adrianna affection, Mary smiled to herself and couldn't remember the last time she had seen her friend this happy. The new man must be great in bed she thought to herself.

"I have so much to fill you in on. I know we talk all the time, but I wanted to tell you some things. I have decided which path I am going to take. I am so glad you are here; I have never been happier." Feeling like a kid all over again when you tell your best friend a secret. Adrianna had to try to remember to breathe she was so excited.

"Ad slow down! I'm not going anywhere and you're talking so fast I can't understand you. I have lots of things to tell you, too. I was just waiting until I came back to town to fill you in." Laughing with her friend Mary felt like she had made the right decision going to Adrianna's house.

Grabbing a cup of coffee and sitting down on the couch, it felt like old times. Adrianna missed having Mary so close, was grateful she was home. Someone she could confide in and tell anything too.

"How long are you here for? You have to stay with me?"

"Actually, I am moving back for good, and I bought a condo about fifteen minutes from here." Mary knew that she wasn't entirely lying, she did have a condo not far away, she just never really left. She had

74

always made sure that Ad had just called her cell phone.

"You're coming home, I can't believe it. This is truly been a day of surprises." Smiling from ear to ear she felt like the pieces of her broken puzzle were being put back together.

"Why Ad, what else has happened? You're smiling like a child who just got the present they asked Santa for." Seeing a definite change in her friend appearance, her confidence was back and that made Mary happy.

"Where to begin? So much has happened in the last couple of months, my life has completely changed" having no clue how her friend was going to take the information, but she couldn't wait to tell her.

"Tell me, come on don't hold back." after seeing her with that man last night, she needed to know what was going on, and that Adrianna was going to be safe.

"My father had hired people to find me after my mother had me. It turns out that she left him and not the story that she told me. All of her stories were not true. Or after so many years of telling them, she believed them herself, I'm not sure. Anyhow, his lawyers found me and told me that he left me money. We aren't talking small change either; I will never have to worry about anything again. I quit my job after taking almost six weeks to cash the check, I just couldn't process that this was actually happening to me."

"How did they find you?" Mary didn't like the way this was going, Adrianna shouldn't have been that easy to find, something must have happened.

"Let's just say they have friends in high places."

"Ok, keeping going, you have made me curious now." High places, wasn't the least of it. How did they find her? Mary made sure that she was always hidden. So many questions came to mind, and she wasn't sure if she was going to like the answers.

"So, I quit my job and decided to take the path less travelled. To start living my life and not being the shell of a person that I have been. The lawyer who came to tell me about my father; well let's just say, that we have become close."

"How close is close?" This must have been the man she was with last night Mary thought to herself.

"We can say, because of him I have a new found respect for living. The best part is, he knew my father. I can't wait for you to meet him; he should be back soon. But enough about me, what have you been doing?"

"Same old stuff; just need a change of surroundings, decided that it was time to come home." Seeing how happy her friend was at the moment, whatever the lawyer is doing he'd better keep it up. She hadn't seen Ad this excited about anything in years. She was acting like she had a school girl crush.

"Can I ask you something Mary?"

"Go ahead, you can ask me anything."

"How do you look the exact same since the last time I've seen you? You haven't aged a day?"

"Well, neither have you. You look great! Still the same Ad, lots of questions; just a smile on your face now."

Looking at Adrianna, she knew her immortality had set in, her flawless looks frozen in time. Mary had to wonder if her friend had ever noticed.

"Come on Mary, you still look the exactly the way you looked when we met. I know that you are only a few years older than me, but you look great. What is your secret?"

"Let's just chalk it up to good genetics." She been avoiding the question for years, while Ad was growing up. Hiding behind makeup but it was just too irritating to wear and eventually she gave it up. She could have used magic, but didn't want to draw attention to herself.

"Mary there is more to it than that, would you tell me already? But hold that thought, I am going to get some more coffee."

Rising off the couch to head to the kitchen, Adrianna was getting de ja vu happening again, but couldn't figure out why? She just knew that

Luc would be arriving at any moment and couldn't wait for the two of them to meet. Hearing a knock at the door, her heart rate began to speed up, she could feel the blush creep across her cheeks. If this was what love felt like, she'd take it by the boat loads.

"Mar, can you grab that for me, I'll be out in a moment."

"Not a problem. Sure." This must be the lawyer, Mary thought to herself.

Opened the door, staring she couldn't believe who was standing in front of her. It had been more years than she could remember, but she wouldn't forget that face anywhere.

"Luc, how are you dear cousin," whispering low enough so Ad couldn't hear.

"Mary! What the hell! Why are you here? You need to leave now before she comes in here."

"What and ruin the surprise? You have some explaining to do Luc so start." Crossing her arms over her chest, seeing the panic stricken look on his face was priceless; she'd enjoy it for the moment. With her back against the door frame; contemplating what to do next.

"I have explaining to do, you disappeared over three hundred years ago, and I need to explain why I am here?" Luc was fuming now. What was she doing here? He needed to know, trying to find Adrianna to make sure that she was safe.

"Hey, Luc come in I see you have already met my friend Mary. Mary let me introduce you to Luc, um, my friend." Adrianna watched as the two of them glared at each other.

"We have already met, actually. I have known Luc for years." That should wipe that smug look off his face Mary thought to herself.

"Yea, you could say Mary and me go way back." He was going to get her for this one, how was Ad going to handle this? Well, there was only one way to find out.

"Adrianna, Mary and I are cousins, I just wasn't aware that she was back in town."

"What a small world, huh Luc, meeting like this after so many years. I can't wait to catch up." And boy, were they going to catch up she said as she punched him in the arm.

"How are you two related?"

"Our mothers were sisters, but I haven't seen my aunt since I was a child." That much Mary could say was true, she had not seen any of her family since she was young. Her mother kept her from them, said it was safer.

"Oh, then you don't know."

"Don't know what Luc?" Ok, now Mary was the confused one.

"My parents disappeared when I was about ten and uncle Sal raised me with his kids, but then several years later his daughter and son left and it was just the two of us." Not wanting to tell her too much information Luc figured that she at least deserved to know this.

"Luc, I am so sorry, I had no idea. How did this happen?" Knowing deep down that Sirena had something to do with this. His parents were good people and would never just leave their son to go somewhere. That just didn't make sense, but Luc was so young when they left, and he never knew the side of Sirena that she did.

"They were just going to go for a weekend away and were never heard from again. Uncle Sal looked for a long time, but nothing ever turned up."

As Luc and Mary looked at one another, they knew that this discussion was far from Done. That they would talk about it later when Ad wasn't around.

The humming of energy through the air, Adrianna knew that there was something more going on. Sensing that there was more to come, the ride they were about to embark on would be one filled with bends and curves, and she was up for the challenge. With the strange silence emanating from them both, as much as she wanted to say 'just tell me already', Adrianna wasn't entirely sure she wanted to know. Leaving them to sit back on the couch, she figured they'd join when they were ready.

Whispering quietly enough that her friend could hear, Mary

knew what needed to be done. It was too late to keep Adrianna in the dark, she had already changed, and now with Luc in her life she would have more support to help her. Having spent years protecting Adrianna she wasn't about to have everything blow up in her face.

"How did you guys find her?"

"What! How did we find her? What are you doing with her? Didn't you think to let someone else know, like her father? Uncle Sal has been going crazy looking for her."

"I've been keeping her safe dear cousin, which is more than I can say for you. Making sure that no one hurt her or her mother again, keeping them protected and hidden from our world."

"Protected from who? Her family, all these years should could have known her father, but you choose not to say anything? Why?" His cousin had the answers he had searched so long for, he wasn't going to let her off that easily.

"Her family? That's rich, that's who I was protecting her from. Since the first time that I met her mother at the clinic something had been up. I was there when Adrianna was born, I could feel the magic in the air. Someone was out to hurt them, her mother remembered nothing except what they wanted her to. Not knowing who was after them, I did everything I could to keep her safe, I didn't trust anyone."

"Then why leave Adrianna to fend for herself? Why leave?"

"She kept question me, why I never aged. I never left town, I checked on her every day, she just never knew."

"So dearest cousin, where does that leave us now? Adrianna doesn't know a thing about her immortality. Doesn't even know how old I am. So, if you're so smart Mary, what do we do now?"

"She's not going to understand about us, not right away. She needs to find out slowly, if we work together, we can do this."

"Don't you think you've done enough cousin." The words dripped with distain from his lips.

"Nice, macho bullshit. Get over yourself. She will trust me a hell of a lot more than you Luc."

"Fine, tell her slowly, but I'll be the one to do it, not you. She's mine and that's…."

"You didn't? Please tell me you didn't Luc."

"Didn't what?"

"You know damn well what I'm talking about! How could you!"

"Because keeping her safe is more important to me than anything."

"She isn't going to be happy."

"Then she doesn't need to know until later."

"Fine, but I want front row seats when she knocks your head off. Your such an ass."

"It's a family trait, your family, so get over it." Raising an eyebrow, making sure his point got across.

Walking past his cousin to where Adrianna was seated. He should have expected Mary to swoop in, sitting right next to her. It pissed him off and she knew it too. Taking the seat across from Adrianna, he wanted nothing more than Mary to leave. It looked like she was in it for the long run. His day he had planned with Adrianna just went down in flames.

With the tension growing in the air, even Adrianna was aware there was more going on than she first thought. There was something between them, knowing that they would tell her when they were ready. She still didn't like the tension she felt.

With idle conversations filling up the next few hours, Mary left to go home. There was too much left unsaid that needed to be dealt with. Luc could find her and then they could take it from there. Curious to know why her friend kept referring to her father in the past though, wondering what exactly Luc had told her.

Adrianna wasn't going to like the fact her cousin promised forever to her either. Luc had just married her for eternity, smirking to herself thinking of what Ad would do when she found out. Mary didn't want to miss that show for anything, it would be the best entertainment she'd had in centuries.

All those years, trying to keep Adrianna safe; could she have been wrong? Maybe she should have consulted Fate on her opinion, or the elders. She didn't know who to trust. She wouldn't roll over now like some wolf. She had kept her friend hidden for her own safety. Adrianna had skirted danger more times than she could count. Deep down knowing what she did was right.

Luc would be there soon, together she hoped that they could keep Adrianna safe. There was more going on here than either of them first thought.

Making an excuse to leave Adrianna's, he told her he had to head back to the office to finish some paperwork. Hating having to leave her, but needed to talk to Mary to figure out what had been going on. What had his cousin been thinking all these years. He had to get answers.

Reaching his cousins condo, the same feeling as the day before crept over him, as if he was being watched. Everything seemed normal, maybe he was just overreacting he thought. To be safe he took the elevator to her condo. Maybe she knew something they didn't, he needed to find out.

With a sharp knock at the door, she knew he had arrived. Why he hadn't flashed in was beyond her. Not wanting to waste any time, the situation needed to be handled properly and fast. The one thing about her family was they couldn't lie very well. They all had tells, so getting the truth wouldn't be difficult, and neither of them wasted any time.

Arguing back and forth was getting them nowhere. With each of them believing they knew what was best for Adrianna, the conversation was like a revolving door.

"This is ridiculous Mary, you've been hiding her, and we've been looking for her. Where getting nowhere at all."

"I told you, when Nina came into the clinic pregnant, something seemed off. When I knew the baby was like us what else was I supposed to do?"

"The fact that her mother lied to her for years, leaves no bearing on you what so ever does it?"

"Don't you find it strange? A woman, ready to give birth comes into a clinic, and according to how 'we' do things the father wasn't around. You know our history, what father would do that, risk that in a human hospital?"

"Fine, point taken, then what do you think happened? How did you hide her for over a century and make her forget?"

"I knew something was off so I interceded. I followed her and her mother around, always keeping hidden so they would be safe. Wait…A century? It's only been over twenty years."

"A century she's been missing. That we can worry about later. How did you hide the fact you don't age for years?"

"Make up and wigs mostly, when it became too much of a bother, I just pretended to be the niece of the older lady so I didn't have to hid so much.

"How did you keep her hidden so well? She went to public school, and worked in town. We had everyone looking for her."

"I camouflaged her. It was the only spell I was willing to do all these years. It took time to perfect but it worked wonderfully. You would have walked past her a hundred times and never seen her unless she wanted to be seen. The humans could see her perfectly, but our kind couldn't. It was the only way to keep her safe." Sensing the confusion in him, Mary explained how it came to her.

Growing up she was always sent to her aunts and grandmothers, to learn the arts as they called it. There was good and evil in the world, for every ounce of one, there was the exact opposite in the other. For all the goodness they held, there was an equal amount of evil. Having been given the gifts of healing and goodness, she stared at her cousin as he registered who the evil would have been. As if a spark had been lit the name rolled off his tongue.

"Serina."

"Yep, for all of our goodness, she is pulsating with evil. Her mother and their family cultivated her. Making her more powerful than her predecessors, until they didn't know what to do with her any more. Why do you think her mother kept pushing uncle Sal to marry her? If they would have committed Serina would have her full powers and then none of us could ever have stopped her. Without their union, she only has a fraction, and even that is beyond measure."

"So, you're basically saying that Serina is the devil incarnate, and it's up to us to stop her."

"Not us, Adrianna, she's the only one who can do it, and she doesn't even know what she is capable of. I know she has powers, but I can't figure them out. Just recently they started to loosen up, that's how I guess you found her. I never figured out who was after them. I just had to keep them safe."

"How exactly is Adrianna more powerful than us, if she doesn't even know who or what she is? That makes no sense?"

"Uncle Sal, is extremely powerful, with the exception of her grandmother. But by not loving Serina and Sebastian's mother, he didn't pass anything on to them. That's why Serina rebelled so much. Since he had unconditional love for Adrianna's mother, it all went to her. Passed down along the line. Love makes it stronger. But she has no idea. I was coming home to tell her and start training her. Then I opened the door and there you were. Talk about a wrench in the plans. That still doesn't tell me why you are here and with her? She is going to

kill you when she finds out that you wed her without her knowing. You know that?"

"Yes, I know. But it was the only way I knew to keep her safe, to know where she is always. Uncle Sal, looked for her for years. He wants to give her everything she ever wanted. When I finally found her, she was so lost and alone. I left her with the check and a way to reach me. But I was on my way to see her, when she came to my office. I couldn't stay away; I knew that she was the one for me. She was mine. I was going to make sure of that. I have to go to the office; we can finish this later. Sal could be back anytime wanting answers."

Knowing that his desk would be piled high for all the work he missed the last few day, he had to catch up before his boss found out. As Luc entered the office his boss was already there. Staring right at him through the glass walls was Mr. G, the man didn't look happy either.

"How was your time away?"

"You know very well, how my damn couples of days were Luc. So, stop pussy footing around."

"Sir, I am not quite sure that I understand what you're getting at? You left in such a 'poof', let's say, that there wasn't much to be desired. And may I remind you, humans use doors, and your vanishing acts are getting harder and harder to cover up. Unless you are going to put up dark glass walls, everyone can see in, remember?"

"Does it look like I really give a shit whether or not they can see me? After the bomb you dropped on me the other day, walking out of here wasn't an option. What the hell? You tell me that she never knew that her father wanted her. And I was supposed to be alright with that? For the life of me, my tolerance isn't that angelic and you of all people......"

"Sir. Really, I understand" ...but after he tells him the rest, he may as well bend over and kiss his own ass goodbye he thought..."some other circumstances have brought themselves to my attention. And it is best that you are made fully aware of the entire situation." Luc knew he was going to be pissed, but what was he going to do. If he could deal with his boss, he could handle Adrianna, he hoped.

"WHAT OTHER SITUATION? I have been through the wringer and back in the last seventy-two hours, what else could have possibly happened? And if you even leave out a detail, I won't care if you're my nephew or not, your ass will be mine."

"Fine, then have a seat uncle; because what I told you before is going to seem like a frickin walk through the park", Luc knew that this was going to be a long morning, he just hoped that Adrianna was enjoying hers.

For the next couple of hours, he told his uncle the updated version of the story. Luc would have thought if there was ever a chance of hell freezing over, it probably just happened. The amount of energy radiating off his uncle was unparalleled. The tension could be felt in the air, ever immortal in the office could feel it. He was sure a few of the humans could as well. It was like a fog creeping off the ocean on the warm spring morning. Thick and dense, you knew that there were things around you but you, just couldn't see them. Never in all his existence had he ever felt such a strong emotion. The vibrations in the room were overwhelming, everyone in the building must have been able to feel it, because everyone cleared the floor. His uncle was one person you didn't want to piss off even on a good day.

As if a storm had passed, his uncles eyes began to clear. The stormy blue sea colour was replaced by a crisp blue. Watching as his nephew tried to read his emotions. If he felt betrayed or relieved, about how Mary handled the situation. He was torn, part of him wanting to rip her apart and the other half wanted to coddle her with praise. As if she was a child who put away a toy without being asked too.

Who could have been the threat? Who could have done such a sadistic and cruel thing, to an unborn child? Ripping a family apart for no apparent reason, other than for one's pleasure. He has witnessed a lot of things in his time of earth; but this by far was one of the most, malicious. Being directed toward someone he knew, maybe, but there had to be more he wasn't sure. He would get to the bottom of it, until the last breath was wrought from his body. Whoever this person was, there weren't going to like dealing with him that he was assured of.

Nobody likes to deal with Mr. G, he was too much like his mother and everyone avoided her.

"Luc, I want you to find out everything Mary has put together. Tell her that I want her in my office tomorrow morning. And if she doesn't want to come, tell her too bad. Our first priority is to keep Adrianna safe. She needs to learn the truth about herself or this will just get that much worse."

"Alright uncle, I will let Mary know. I will keep a close eye on Adrianna. We will get to the bottom of this. Can you use the door, not the other way please. They have all seen you in here, it just makes my life easier."

"Tomorrow I will have the glass replaced and solve that little issue. Just remember, keep her safe. I have some searching to do myself. Adrianna still doesn't need to know everything, leave me out of it for now. That, she can learn at her own pace."

"Agreed."

Watching his uncle used the front door for once, he agreed with him. The less Adrianna knew about his uncle, the better off she was, for now. He couldn't keep it a secret forever.

CHAPTER SEVEN

Pacing in circle, Serina couldn't figure out what had gone wrong. They were meant to be together. She had made sure that no one ever got close. It was part of the spell; he wasn't supposed to be with anyone except her. What in the hell had happened? Swiping her arm across the shelf in a fit of rage, all the trophies came crashing to the floor. A sinister smile crept over her lips as she stared at them laying there in a heap. The pleasure of hurting them brought her solace.

The years she wasted, for what? Maybe the woman was just a client or business partner? But why go to her home? She'd be damned if she let some two-bit whore ruin everything. Relishing in the memories of the past and all the misery she brought, it wouldn't be long before she brought this woman down.

Tormenting her father was just for fun. He'd ruined everything when he wouldn't promise forever to her mother. The power that she would have had if they did would have been unimaginable. But, for now she held all the power; all the power was hers for the taking and nothing would trump her hand. She kept her cards close and playing them carefully.

With a wave of her hand everything was back in its place, no worse for ware, except one. All the power they brought her, the misery she instilled into them. If they could talk, the world would really know what kind of monster she really was. Pulling one off the shelf and holding it her hand, Serina stared into its depths. That one trophy in particular, if that were ever fell into the wrong hands; shaking her head at the thought. Serina knew that the trouble she had caused, would be nothing compared to what she would receive in return.

"You know that you are never going to be free. You know that right." Telling the trophy as she put it back on the shelf. That one had been the most work. The months of staying with her grandmother. Just to ensure that there would be a means to an end. If her grandmother only knew her original intention, she would have never let Serina stay with her. The coddling, and putting up with the old witch, and she never had a clue. Smirking to herself as she placed it back on the shelf. The misery it radiated only fueled her. The more she suffered, the stronger Serina became drawing on the powers.

Watching her grand-daughter leave, the woman smiled to herself. There was a greater plan at work. She had been willing to be the sacrifice, it meant the future would be set on the right path. When she returned, paying her grand-daughter a visit would be one of the first things she would do. Fate and Destiny worked hand in hand and she liked to keep them both real close.

Closing her eyes, letting herself drift off into a healing sleep, needing to recharge her already damaged body. Knowing that the time would come soon, feeling the magical energies that had shifted in the realm.

"It has begun." She sighed and drifted off to sleep.

AWAKEN THE FLAMES

CHAPTER EIGHT

A fresh layer of powdered snow blanketed the roof of her car; the crisp air burning her lungs as she drew each breath. Sensing a new, vibrant world, a smile curved the corners of her mouth. If this was what love was like she would take it any day. Feeling free to conquer the world for the first time in years with no worries as to what the future may hold. Today she thought would be the spark of new beginnings.

Heading towards her car, staring at the thin layer of ice that coated the walkway, she knew it would be interesting getting to her car. Ice and Adrianna never mixed well, as firm as it looked before her; it always melted the closer she came to it. With each gingerly laid step, she could see the red shine of her car calling her. The cougar had served her well over the years, but knew that it was time for a rest. The temperamental vehicle could now be replaced with a more reliable one.

The soft snow carelessly fell from the car as she brushed it off, the excitement of the day was surging like fire through her veins. Unable to remember the last time she had ever bought something so luxurious for herself. Turning the key in the ignition, as if the car knew what was in store, it refused to spark to life. As the chirping of the alternator informed her that this would be its final resting place and refused to move.

Reaching in her pocket for her cell, she dialed Mary's number hoping that her friend could help. Adrianna knew that it would give them a chance to catch up as well. With no escape, her friend would have to answer her questions.

With her phone vibrating in her pocket, Mary was shocked to see Adrianna calling so early. Hoping nothing was wrong she wasted no time in answering the call.

"Hi Mary, I know you just got back to town, but I could really use a favor. The cougar finally went to a better place, and I need to get a new car. I thought maybe you could help and we could spend the day together?"

"It's about time you got rid of that pile of scrap metal!"

"Hey! It's my pile of scrap metal so lay off." Sharing a laugh with her friend.

"I'll come get you, but your buying lunch after!"

"Fine, you twisted my rubber arm. See you soon."

"That way I can have you to myself and my dear cousin can't find us, you'll be all mine!"

"I see we still haven't grown up. Just come get me already. I'll be waiting with bells on."

"Bells? Listen I really don't need to know what you and Luc are into alright. The less I know the better!" Hanging up the phone Mary wasted no time going to Adrianna's house.

Pacing around the house waiting for her friend, she had so many questions coming to mind, unsure of where to start, but today Adrianna wanted answers. Mary had been hiding something for years. She knew it with every fiber of her body. Just what it was, she didn't know. But knew today she would find out. Pushing her friend for answers in the past never really worked, just ended up causing more question. Today was going to be different she thought to herself.

Feeling the blood flowing through her veins. Warming her, bringing her power, letting the slow pulsing let warmth flow through her body, easing any stress she had out of her muscles. Sensing her friend was she headed outside to see her. The feeling of knowing when things were going to happen was growing more with each day. Adrianna just wishing she would have had the trick in high school before a surprise test, or final exams.

Slipping into the plush leather heated seats of Mary's car, she knew what her first upgrade would be. With toasty warm buns any day would be a great day she thought to herself.

"Hey, how did you know that I was going to be her so soon? What were you waiting in the cold the whole time?"

"I just knew that you were about to pull up that's all."

"That's it? You just knew? Does that happen often?" Mary knew that explaining would come faster than she thought. Too many things were happening to fast to her friend and she knew that her dear cousin was to blame for the sudden spike in her powers.

"It started after mom died, I guess it's just her way of watching over me, but it has been happening more over the last few days. Like when the phone rings, if I concentrate, I know who it is before I answer it; but if I'm rushing, I have no idea. Like an early warning system or something. Why?"

"No reason, just wondering."

"Hey Mary, thanks for getting me today, but can we talk, I mean really talk."

"Sure, what's up? Why so serious? Can it wait though? I forgot something at my place and I'd really like to show it to you."

Reversing the car out of the driveway, Mary knew that the time had come, she knew the questions her friend would ask. She just hoped she'd be as ready, for the answers she was going to get. Her friend's life had already been turned upside down once. Her answers were only going to cause more questions. When Adrianna finds out about Luc, she wasn't going to be happy. That one would be his problem, she thought to herself.

Taking the ramp from the highway, and coasting through the

streets of the city it wasn't long till they reached Mary's home. The top of the building shrouded in the falling snow; a chill crept up Adrianna's spine. Shaking it off Ad followed her friend inside. As they entered the building, a light marble floor greeted them. With a small waterfall that emptied into an oval shaped pool. Walking past and looking at all the coins, thinking about all the wishes that had been made as adults and children walked past. Reaching into her pocket for loose change, she couldn't help herself. As if knowing what she was looking for, Mary handed her a penny she saw on the floor, the head was facing up. Pass it along and they would both have good luck.

Silently making a wish and holding the coin against her heart, Ad tossed it into the fountain. Knowing that what her wish for was impossible, she didn't care. If she only ever had this one wish to ask, it was going to be a good one.

"What did you wish for Adrianna?" Mary asked even though she already had a pretty good idea.

"Nothing really, but if I tell you it won't come true. And some wishes are worth waiting for."

Adrianna knew that better than anyone.

As the elevator doors opened into the foyer of the home, it was just as Adrianna pictured the place her friend lived. Warm and inviting warping you in a hug and making you feel welcomed the instant you step foot into it.

It was just how she thought her friend would live, very simple. A cream-colored carpet on the floor. All the furniture had clean lines, and seemed to flow as if they were meant to be together. Nothing from one set though, more of a miss match of designs, but they worked. A few oil paintings hung on the walls, a glass vase with fresh flowers here and there. The kitchen was a clean cream color with a light marble finish and an under-mount sink. Her bedroom had a view to die for. It overlooked the park and, in the distance, you could see a glimpse of the lake. Just enough, to make it tranquil. The walls were a cream with powder blue accents. It all worked.

Taking a seat on the couch, Mary offered a cup of tea, which she couldn't refuse. Adrianna knew the more comfortable her friend was, the more likely she would be to answer her questions. Accepting the cup. Tucking her legs beneath her she waited, seeing her friend seated comfortably beside her, knowing the timing was right.

"So, Mary, are you going to tell me or do I have to pry it out of you?"

"Tell you what?"

"WHAT? You know what? The only question you've been avoiding for years? What is it? Botox? A little lipo? Or something else? Come on, don't hold out on me."

"I told you, good genes. And not the ones on my ass either, before you ask that next."

"I wouldn't have dared. What are you wearing these days anyway…or are you going to make me looked?" Leaning forward on the couch she asked her friend.

Missing the fun that they were having. Adrianna couldn't remember the last time she had laughed this much. Positive that laughed more in the last three days, than she had in years. If this was going to keep up, she would be the one needing the lipo sooner than later.

"I don't know if you are going to like what I am going to say. You have to promise not to say anything to anyone. Keep an open mind because everything I am going to tell you will, seem a little weird, but it is the truth."

"Now you have really peeked my interests."

Since as a child you were always told to jump into the pool with both feet, because one step at a time was just delaying what was going to happen. Right then and there, seeing that Adrianna was sitting on the couch; Mary decided the only way to tell her was by disappearing. So.....Why in the hell wasn't she answering the phone? Luc had already called Mary three times and nothing, only the answering service. With each message, he was getting more pissed. Deciding to try Adrianna next, he didn't have a good feeling about any of this today.

"Hey Ad, it's me Luc. Just was wondering if you would like to join me for dinner later? Let me know." Why did he feel like a sixteen-year-old for some reason? This woman was slowly going to be the death of him, he just knew it. He may be a lawyer, but she made him feel like a kid again, and that was a long, long time ago. Not really wanting to go back and visit, one trip through puberty was enough for anyone.

The way she made him feel, as if being awaken from darkness you never knew existed; she had done this for him. He thought all these centuries that he lived. His life only truly began the moment he laid eyes on her. His wife, no one could ever change that. Adrianna was going to be with him forever.

Luc could picture the happiness that they would share as a couple. The joy their children would bring into their lives. An eternity with the one you were made for. They complimented each other. His strengths and hers fit so well. He was logical, she free. He'd had only known her for a few weeks, each time he thought of Adrianna, it was as if a whole new world was laid at his feet. He didn't want to waste a minute of it. Life for him had truly just begun. His uncle didn't need to know what was going on yet. He had to deal with Mary first, and Adrianna still had to find out who she really was.

His uncle really needed to meet with Mary today, knowing that she was purposely, not answering her cell. Well, he would just keep bugging her until she did. She couldn't avoid him all day. Walking through the halls of the office, he needed to find a place to vanish.

Just needed to make sure that everything was alright. Luc's senses were going off on full volume for some reason. He didn't like the feeling that he was getting because of it. Mary was up to something; he just didn't know what.

"Mary. MARY. MARY. What the hell?" not knowing what was happening, Adrianna began to panic. Where did her friend go? This wasn't funny, too many weird things were happening and this was on the top of the list.

Turning around frantically, she looked everywhere for her friend. "Ok, Mar, that is enough. Ha, ha, ha nice magic trick, now get out here!". What was going on?

"Turn around Ad, I am right here" Mary knew that this was going to take a while.

"What in the hell was that? And when did you go all Vegas on me?"

"You might want to sit down again Adrianna; this is going to take a while." She was putting it lightly, and Mary didn't know where to begin.

"Can you please tell me what is going on? What the hell that was that you just did?" Answers, she needed answers and had to be patient with herself. Who was she fooling; that would never happen. Feeling as if her temperature was rising by the minute, she needed to relax.

"There is a lot about me that you don't understand Ad, but you need to know. You are a lot like me, you just don't know it yet."

"Mary, what are you talking about? How am I a lot like you? And why are you looking at me like that? You're the one who did the vanishing act." Seeing the halo of color surrounding her friend, there was more going on with Ad than even Mary was ready for.

"Like I said, this might take a while, so let's have seat and go from there please. Ad, you know that you can trust me." Please don't scorch my couch was all she could think seeing a red glow radiating around her friend, who was completely unaware.

Adrianna knew that she could trust her friend, however vanishing was not something she expected. Plastic surgery yes. This, this was something entirely different. If Mary could do this, and her and Luc were cousins. There were so many things going on in her head right now, she wasn't sure that she really wanted all the answers to the questions that she had. But, knew that she needed to hear them.

"Mary, this better be good. What's with all the suspense, just tell me already."

"Just don't judge me, and understand everything I did was for a reason. The two of us we are different, from everyone else in the world. You just never realized how different we are. You're not part of this world, not really anymore. You have changed a lot in the last several years, and are now part of something bigger."

106

"Stop beating around the bush, and tell me. First, why you do still look the same as I always Remember. Second what the hell was that earlier?"

"Are you ready? Really, ready for the truth? Because your world will change! I am not really sure that you are ready, for everything I am about to tell you."

"Just spill it already." Not entirely sure if she really wanted to hear everything here friend was about to say, but Adrianna wanted to hear the truth. She needed to hear the truth, no matter what.

"Your first question is why don't I look any older? That's because I stopped aging when I was a teenager, like all immortals. It's like we freeze in time. Like you, I am a witch. I have been watching over you all your life. Keeping you safe and hidden so that no one could hurt you, or your mother. I don't know how she became ill because that wassn't supposed to happen..." Realizing the look on her friends face, Mary thought that she would give Ad a moment, to absorb things.

"A witch! You expect me to believe that? Come on Mary. Really, I wasn't born yesterday. You need a better story than that." Too in shock to think of anything else, it wasn't possible that things like witches didn't exist.

"Adrianna, why would I lie? You asked me for the truth. And I am telling you the truth. I am a witch, that's all. Not lying, I am what I am. And so are you. Don't you realize, that you haven't change over the last several years? That you look the exact same! You said yourself that you are sensing when things are about to happen. When you know something bad is coming, you want to protect yourself."

"But everybody senses things. People have a sixth sense about this. I don't believe you. Show me something, come on, give it your best shot."

"What. Like this?"

Adrianna was staring in awe. There in the palm of her friend's hand was a glowing ball of light. Energy was radiating up her arms a completely surrounding her. Scooting back on the couch, not wanting to believe what she was seeing, she had just remembered something.

"Um, Mary, you said that you, and um and Luc were cousins, right? Does that mean that he is........he is like you?"

"Yes Ad. Luc is a witch, and a powerful one. Not as powerful as you, but powerful nonetheless. The light that you are staring in shock at is energy. I can control it for protection and strength. Didn't you always seem to feel more secure when I was around? That's what my ability is, protecting those around me. I can sense when harm is near."

"So, hold on. You're telling me I am immortal and a witch? That I have these powers, that I don't even know about? Come on Mar, are you for real? I am not a witch; I would know if things were different. I would just know? And wait, you said you stopped aging. Exactly how old are you?" Ad wasn't sure that she really wanted to know, but she had to ask.

"Let's just say that I have a few centuries on you, three plus a few more years."

"YOU'RE HOW OLD? O.M.G, wait. If your over three hundred years, then exactly how old is your cousin? Wait, don't answer that, I am not sure that I really want to know." Could this day get any weirder? What else could possible happen?

"Ad. Ad, how are you? You're looking a little pale. Come on, answer me." Watching her friend lean forward and holding the edge of the couch, Mary knew that it was a lot to take in. After all she had grown up knowing about witchcraft. She couldn't imagine what Adrianna must be going through at the moment.

"Just give me a second; it's a lot to absorb. It's not every day that you find out that your best friend is a witch. Immortal, oh let's not forget, you're over three hundred years old. And I don't even want to know how old Luc is. Just wait till I get ahold of him."

"Don't be mad at him Ad. He wanted to be the one to tell you. I just thought that you would take it better coming from me. Since I have known you since the day you were born."

She filled Adrianna in on the story that she told Luc. How she was in the delivery room when she was born, and knew that she was different. How she followed her mother around to keep them safe. Knowing that witches weren't usually born in public clinics, and that someone was definitely up to no good. Mary had to make sure that she stayed safe.

The part that Mary tried to avoid was the fact that Adrianna's mother should never have gotten sick. She did everything in her power to keep her hidden and safe. Something didn't add up though, and she would get to the bottom of it.

"Hey Mar, I am getting that feeling again. The one I get just before something is about to happen." At least Adrianna knew that she could trust her instincts. Well, she hoped she could at least.

"Can you guess who it is going to be because things are about to get interesting." Man, is Luc going to be pissed. She owed her friend the truth, and Ad did ask Mary thought to herself.

Deciding to pop in and see his dear cousin who didn't want to answer her cell, he couldn't wait to get ahold of her. What Luc didn't expect was to see Adrianna sitting there on the couch, as if she was waiting for him. The look in her eyes said that she knew. This wasn't going to be an easy thing to explain. Seeing the confusion, and hurt in her eyes, he just wanted to hold her. Telling that she needed space, and was trying to absorb everything.

"Um, Ad, how did you? Why are you? Mary?" he sounded like a tongue-tied child.

"She knows Luc. Well, she knows what she is and who we are. I thought that I would leave the rest to you; and I think that I will give you some time, I'll leave you two alone for a bit"

Mary decided it was time to vanish out of sight. Heading back to Ad's was a good place to go. At least, she could check things out, and see if anything or anyone turns up. Mary had a feeling that she knew who was up to no good. But the question of the moment was: where's the witch, and what is she up to?

AWAKEN THE FLAMES

CHAPTER NINE

Raising her hand so Luc would know she needed space. Adrianna needed to understand everything she had just learned. There was just so much, she was beginning to feel overwhelmed, and relieved at the same time. Having wanted answers to lingering questions, but floored by what she learned. Watching Luc staring, the anxiety on his face, she could tell that he was struggling at the moment. Hell, so was she. He could wait while she processed everything. Taking a few deep breaths and slowing her heart rate, until she was able to speak to him.

"Hiya, Luc. Nice appearing act. Do you have anything that you would care to tell me? Like the fact that you are a witch...and exactly how old are you? What's your specialty?"

Standing up from the couch, not sure if she wanted to be near him or not at the moment. She began pacing in circles around the room. Her nerves were getting the better of her. It was one thing for Mary to tell her what she was. But, to find out Luc was too. Ad didn't think that Luc was too happy about the fact that she knew. Oh well c'est la vie. Rubbing her hands up and down her arms, feeling the heat surrounding her. Feeling like she could breathe again.

"I see that my cousin has filled you in on a few things. Why don't we start with what she has told you, and go from there." Taking a step towards her he stopped himself as he sensed her unease.

"Well, let's see. Mary is a witch, she is immortal, and is centuries old. Has been watching over, and protecting me since the day I was born. She was never far away. Even when she moved, she checked in on me every night. She wasn't sure how my mother had gotten sick, because she was protected. You are her cousin and a witch; she wouldn't elaborate on how old you really are. So come on Luc, dish. I think I should know how old the man I am sleeping with is, don't you?" Ad had not wanted to sound snarky, but she couldn't help it.

"As Mary told you I stopped aging just like you did. So really, we're both the same age, relatively speaking. You could say that I am a little younger than my cousin."

"And exactly what's that magic number?"

"Three hundred and ten years to be exact. Ad, are you alright?" He asked as he watched her sink back down onto the couch. Wanting to reach and help her, hesitating to give her some space at the same time. His emotions were so torn, not knowing what he should do. The court room he could handle, this was something entirely different.

"Yea, yea. I am fine, just a lot for one day. So, is there anything else that you would like to tell me? Anything, fill in the blanks. Feel free, I am sure that I can handle it." Knowing that she really didn't have a choice in handling anything. She just wanted everything out in the open. She had said today was going to be a day for new beginnings.

This day wasn't exactly what she expected.

"Well, like Mary said, she has been protecting you. So that explains why I didn't find you sooner. She is very powerful and had you hidden very well. Whatever the threat was on you and your mother, she used some of her most powerful spells to keep you safe. I just wish I knew who was after you all those years."

"And is there anything else Luc? Are you sure that there isn't anything you are forgetting? If you want to tell and have a clean slate, now is the time." Adrianna knew that there was something else, she just didn't know what. But there had to be more, she could feel it.

"There is more, but I have been asked not to say anything else. My boss would have my head. You will learn everything in time. Please don't rush, something's need to come out in time. Can you understand that?" Knowing that she deserved to know about her father, he couldn't tell her yet; he needed more time. He didn't think she'd relish the fact that they were married according to their laws. That she would find out later, not liking that he tricked her into it. It was the only way to keep her safe. If she decided she didn't want to be married to him, he would have to except it, but would never be able to move on. He knew that they were destined. He just had to make her see it first.

"I will respect that, as long as you're honest with me from now on. No more secrets. Promise no more."

"I swear on my life, I will tell you as much as I can, when I can. I don't want there to be anything between us."

"You're immortal! Life is a long time, but thank you. Can we go somewhere else and talk? That way, Mary can come home."

"How about, we go to my place. I will tell you some more and show you some pictures. Things in view are sometimes easier to seen, than just heard."

"I will just message Mary, so she knows she can come home whenever she wants." She sent Mary a quick message so she knew that she was safe and that she would be with Luc. Buying a car would have to wait she thought, that was now the least of her problems.

"Um, Luc. If you just popped in, and Mary drove me here, how am I supposed to get to your house?"

"Well, you saw how Mary and I can travel, did it not occur to you that you could do the same thing? It will take some practice, but you will get the hang of it. But for now, come here a hold on to me and we can go together."

"You just want to get close to me again." Ad said with a smirk.

"Well, you know any excuse that I can find, now come here and give me a hug."

Before Adrianna knew what happened they were in a different apartment. She knew that it was Luc's, it had his scent all over it. She was going to enjoy this, every minute of it.

Receiving the message from Ad, Mary knew that she had some time to snoop around. Something was definitely off. Someone had been close to here. She knew it with every fiber. What did they want and why Ad? What did she do to warrant this? Whoever this person was, they were being very careful. They knew what they were doing, which never went over well. If they took this much effort in not be traced, they were definitely up to no good. She only knew one person who was the manipulative. Serina! What did that bitch want? She had been gone for centuries. No one has heard a peep from her. Why now? Why Adrianna? Something was off, way off. Finding what it was; was going to take all of her effort.

Serina was trouble incarnate. Everything she touched went to shit. What did Ad have that meant so much to her? Mary was sure that Serina didn't know about Ad. She had hidden her so well. She couldn't possibly know who she was. Could she? There had to be something else. Something that Serina wanted even more than Adrianna.

Mary knew that she was being watched, she felt it in her bones. But she wasn't sure, if she knew about Ad. Maybe she was after someone else. Luc! That's it! Serina wanted Luc, she always wanted him. She might not even know that Adrianna exists. Better not bring it up, but let's see what she wants. This is going to be something that Serina isn't going to expect. 'This should be fun.' Mary muttered before vanishing with a sly smile across her face.

"Where is that whore? And what the hell does she have on Luc; that he follows her around." Serina noticed someone moving inside the house. Trying to visualize better with her mind's eye she knew it wasn't the girl. Wondering who it might be she flashed herself closer trying to get a better look. Ensuring there were no humans in the area. Getting caught would catch the attentions of the group of elders. That being on the bottom of her list of people to see.

"Hello Serina. And what rock did you crawl out from."

"Excuse me, do I know you?"

"No, but I know you. What you are doing here? You have no business here, or anywhere for that matter. So, would you like to tell me, or should I force it out of you?" Mary knew goading her was like playing with fire. The fact that Serina didn't know who she was, or how powerful she was, was to her advantage.

"Why I am here is none of your business. You should leave now while you have a fighting chance."

"Oh, Serina, Serina, Serina. You're still the same old miserable bitch you have always been. I Thought you would've grown up a little in the last few hundred years; but alas, some things never change."

"Listen, I don't know who the hell you are, but this is your last warning. You don't know who you are messing with. I suggest that you leave and don't return." Serina could feel her patience running out. Whoever this witch was, she was about to get up close and personal with her nasty side.

"You don't scare me Serina. First, you're not about to do anything stupid, because Luc would know that you're here. Second you have no clue who I am, or how much power I have. So, drop your 'better than thou attitude' because your shit doesn't fly with me. Leave while you have a chance. Don't ever show your miserable, sorry ass around this town again...if I ever have to repeat myself, your father will know exactly where you are, and how to find you." At the same time Mary hurled a ball of energy at Serina, before she could react, and disappeared. She knew better then to push that witch too far. The energy was like a tracking device that she would never be rid of, no matter how many spells she tried.

"That rotten bitch! JUST WAIT! When I find out who you are, you will be added to my collection just like the rest. I promise you this." Serina cursed under her breath. All she needed was her father to know that she was back. She would deal with him later. She had already made sure his life was in constant turmoil. Though she didn't need a father/daughter reunion just yet; that could wait.

Why was that witch protecting Luc, who was she? Serina wouldn't rest until she found out. She would find out, first things first...where is Luc and who is that girl? Flashing back home she needed to think.

Gazing around her room, the day hadn't gone as she had hoped, but it wasn't over yet, not by a long shot. Having now more questions than answers to fuel her rage, Luc's girlfriend would have another thing coming this time.

"Look at all of you, just wasting away in there. You should've known that I always get what I want, no matter what! How did, you miserable people ever think that you could get passed me. Me! Serina. You're all fools, each and every one of you." Looking at each trophy upon the shelf, they each had their own uses even if they didn't know it yet. As long as they stayed trapped Serina could harness their powers.

"You can't keep us in here forever Serina. Someone is going to find you, and realize everything that you have done. You can't keep hidden forever. You are a real bitch, you know that? When I get free, you will get what is coming to you. Mark my words. Each and every last one of them."

"The way you keep talking, your words aren't going to last much longer. You're as fragile as glass right now and don't you forget it. It's only by chance that you have managed to survive. Whoever was hiding you did a good job, but not good enough. You made on fatal flaw when you made that pledge. But, unfortunately for you, you made it a little too late for anyone that matters to help you." This person was going to drive her around the bend and Serina knew it, but she couldn't be destroyed, not yet. She had promised a friend not to harm her. Why it mattered so much to him, she'd never know, but this one was trouble. If she gets rid of this one, her father will know exactly what she was up to, and where she was, It's way too soon for that. She needed some time to think, leaving her room full of trophies.

"Why do you egg her on like that? You know what she could do to you. Look how long she has had us trapped. Do you really want that for yourself? Whoever it is you're protecting she is going to find out, she always does."

"This is where you are wrong. She will never find out my secret. I spent my entire existence making sure of it. The family who was helping to protect it, is the only one that can help, it was safer for everyone that way. We will be free, mark my words. We will be free, very soon." Choosing to stop talking because, Serina was coming back in the room. If she knew the truth, she would stop at nothing, nothing at all and she had to keep the person safe.

"If all of you would stop talking, it would be wonderful. Your constant chatter is annoying. None of you are ever going to get out of here. The faster you realize it the happier you'll be. Now I am leaving for a bit, and I don't want any trouble. Especially from the three of you, keep it up. If the two of you thought the last couple of centuries have been bad, you haven't seen anything yet."

Now that Serina left, she needed to figure out who that woman was from earlier. She knew that the witch definitely had power. She could feel it radiating off of her. But who was she, and what the hell did she want? She knew that she wanted Luc, but who would know that. And how long had she been watching her? Something else was going on, but what? What was she missing?

Finding things out was going to be hard. She had already been all over town, and her signatures were everywhere. Someone was bound to tap into it and find her. Staying away from her father's business was a must, and anything that was remotely related to him. If he ever knew what had gone on, he would kill her; and that would be putting it mildly. Torture, then death, would be more like it. Considering all the things she had done over the centuries; torture would be right up his way. Knowing what he was capable of, she didn't want to be one of them.

When she finds the witch, she will have another thing coming, that's for sure she thought to herself. Walking around her home, she stopped in front a mirror her mother had given her as a child, it was the one thing that connected her to their world. Mirrors were a means for control for her, staring as if centering herself, "So what am I waiting for?" she muttered to her reflection and disappeared.

\#   \#   \#

With her head a little fuzzy from her first flash, she needed to be clear to back in the game. Adrianna couldn't help but look around at Luc's, he loved all the old things and the stories behind them. Having told her when and where they came from, Adrianna was fascinated by it all. Wondering around, running her fingers along the edges of the furniture, trying to get a feel for the space. This was all his, who he was, his past.

"You know Adrianna; you'll have stuff one day as well. Remember, you're immortal now. You have years to procure everything your heart ever wants. You have enough money to buy your own residence, so that you can come and go as you please. The reason that we choose condo's is because the tenants always change and so do the staff. You can come and go and they never notice. They just keep thinking that it's been willed down, and that a trust pays for the maintenance."

"You really have it all figured out, don't you? But doesn't it get sad? Making friends and then having to leave them before they realize your, I mean, our secret?" Cocking her head to one side, resting against the couch. She knew that he was thinking the best way to answer her question.

"Most of my friends are witches, so they are around as long as I am. You will meet some, and then realize that there are a lot more out there than you think."

"You said before that you tried to find me, but couldn't, and that my father looked for me for years. If you are immortal, shouldn't he be? I thought that immortality meant forever, and that you couldn't die?"

"Partially true. You see we can live forever, but there are ways for us to die. We can die of a broken heart. Once we find our partner and promise forever to them, we are linked. A link so strong that it's nearly impossible to break, but it can happen. Witchcraft is tricky, not all black and white. There are many witches and warlocks out there that mean harm. They can imprison people. Make their partners sick with sadness. Once they think their partner is gone from them forever, they just lose their will to live and slowly begin to vanish. Then eventually they are no more. It's very sad and I have only seen it happen on a few occasions."

"So, is that how my father died?" Thinking that her father had died of a broken heart, was not something she relished in. No one should have to go through that, she could feel her chest tighten at the thought.

"That's where the grey area comes in. See, your mother never really pledged forever to your father, so his heart is intact and...." Realizing what he had said after the fact, he could see the sparks appear in her eyes. Like little flames flickering in the light.

"Hang on, can you repeat that? So, you are saying that my father is still alive. That he isn't dead? I would know, wouldn't I; I should know this." As if struggling with herself, trying to reach out for answers as if they would come to her. Staring at him wondering why he hadn't said so sooner, a glimmer of hope as if a warm hug wrapped itself around her.

"Yes, Adrianna, your father is alive and is dealing with much. He wanted you to have this, but it wasn't supposed to happen till later.

Mary kind of rushed things, which I am going to pay for. He gave me something to give to you." Walking over to the dresser, he picked up the second manila envelopes, and handed it to Adrianna. "I hope that this will explain more to you. I will give you a few moments to read it in private."

Handing her the envelope, he knew that it had in it what she needed to hear. Luc could feel his heart aching for her. He could see the realization sinking in, as she held the paper in her hands. He fought the urge to hold her. With her hand resting on top of his, not wanting to release the envelope. A sheen of tears washing over her eyes, trying to comprehend everything that was going on.

"Luc, please don't leave. If it wasn't for you, I would never have known this. Stay with me, I don't think that I can do this by myself." Hearing the cracking in her own voice, a letter from her father. The emotions in her body were fighting amongst themselves, he could feel her pain as if it were his own.

Looking at her eyes welling up with tears, he reached to comfort her. Holding her in his arms knowing that she was reaching out to him, he decided to stay, it was the least that he could do. Every minute they were together he could feel his heart growing, the love he had for her knew no bounds.

"Just give me a minute. But, could you read it for me, I don't know if I have the strength."

"I would be honored" Luc felt his heart go out to her. He knew that he had done the right thing, when he pledged forever to her.

Holding the envelope, Luc looked into Adrianna's eyes for reassurance. Her head was tilted slightly off to the side, her hair hanging loosely around her shoulders. Looking so innocent and lost, to have her life turned upside down, reality altered. She wanted to know; but was afraid to. He knew that the truth was only going to confuse her more.

Cupping her face, he rubbed the pad of his thumb across her bottom lip. She slowly brought her lower lip beneath her top teeth. Knowing that she was wanting it and shying away at the same time. He made her feel safe, he could feel it. This was what it was about, being there for the one you love. Everything revolved around it, love, happiness, family, brought it all together. He wasn't going to let anyone, or anything, ever hurt Adrianna again. It was a silent vow he made to himself, one he would spend the rest of his life ensuring he'd keep. Luc was her world now, making her feel safe and secure, was what he was all he cared about.

He had spent his whole life waiting for the right women to come into it, for just this reason. Now that he had Adrianna, he was going to make sure that she wanted for nothing ever again. Luc was going to be the one she would always turn to when she needed something. He was going to love every minute of it. Eternity wasn't going to be long enough. Not for the love he already had for her.

"Adrianna, no matter what, know that I am here for you. Can you remember that please?" He said trying to reassure her. She had been through a lot already today; this was just going to add to it.

"I will, I promise. I am ready, can you open it before I change my mind. There has been so much to deal with, I just need to know it all. The whole thing, and please don't leave anything out. I beg you, don't try and spare my feelings. I have been through enough in my life. That's all I want, to know the truth."

Taking a deep breath, she looked up searching for answers in his eyes. There was something there, something she needed and trusted. Brushing her lips into the palm of his hand, and placing a kiss, she waited for him to begin.

My Dearest Daughter,

There is much that you don't understand, and for that, I am sorrier than you could ever imagine. I know that the money I have put aside for you is not much in comparison to growing up without a father. When your mother left me, I searched for her for years; it was like she just disappeared off the face of the earth. And I hired the best in the world to track her down, but no one could come up with anything. It was like she had never existed.

I must believe that you were taken from me for a reason, far greater than I can understand. One day I hope I will know why, but you have a greater purpose. Your future is special and bright. You are meant to do something great, for that, I am certain.

Luc will help you in your journey and keep you safe. Think of him as your own personal guardian, if he is near, you will come to no harm.

There is more about your family that you need to be aware of. When I met your mother, I knew that she was the one for me. I fell in love with her the first moment I laid eyes on her. The fact that she was a mortal did not concern me. If we pledge our love to an immortal and they accept it, we can turn them. We cannot reveal our true selves to them until they pledge their forever. I asked your mother over and over again, but she would not accept. The day that she left, was the day that I received the news of her pregnancy from the doctor and she never returned.

You also need to know that before I was with your mother, I was involved with another of our kind. We had 2 children together and I was never in love with her. There is much to that story and we will get to that later. I just ask that you don't judge me.

Luc can fill you in on the details because it is a story that is better spoken not written.

You have a half-brother named Sebastian who is a wonderful and loving man. He vanished a long time ago and we are still trying to find him. You also have a half-sister named Serina, but now I need you to watch out for her. She is just like her mother and has a nasty streak in her. Now, for your own protection, I never told either of them about you because, quite frankly, I didn't trust Serina. Again, Luc can fill in the details.

Not knowing exactly where you have been, and only learning recently that I have a beautiful daughter, I am very excited to meet you when you are ready. I don't want to pressure you because according to Luc, you have been through a lot in your life. I just wish I was there to help you through it. (Why you and your mother were taken from me I don't know, but now that I found you, I won't stop until I do.)

When you are ready to see me, Luc knows how and where to   find me. Just know that I was never truly far away, just neither of us knew it at the time.

I look forward to the day when you are ready to meet me and will be waiting for you with open arms. My only wish would be that your mother was here with us. I can't help but feel that she is in some way. That she truly never left.

All my love and wishes for you, my most precious daughter

Dad

Placing the letter down on the table, Luc could hear the soft cries. He moved closer to Adrianna. Gently lifted her up into his lap, holding her there. Knowing that it wasn't words that she needed to hear now. She had already heard the story of her siblings and their antics; she needed comfort. She had been alone for so long, and just need to be held and to feel safe. That was one thing that he could do, and always take pleasure in doing for her. He was going to make sure that she always knew that she could run to him for anything.

"I'm sorry, I just need a minute, and it's been a lot in such a short time. My father is alive, I just never thought......I never imagined in all these years that he was looking for me and wanted to see me. That he wanted to keep me safe from my sister. I always had my mother, but never knew, I never knew," she putting her head back on Luc's chest and just letting the warmth soothe her. She felt herself slowly drift off in the comfort of his embrace and he never wanted to leave it.

Lifting Adrianna up and carrying her to the bedroom, Luc knew that she needed to rest and regain her strength. He removed her shoes and gently tucked her beneath the duvet and slid in beside her. She would wake and know that she wasn't alone, no matter what. Knowing that she never realized about the vow she made, that would come in time. First, he would have to deal with the fact that his uncle was going to rip off his head when he finds out what he did. Uncle Sal was going to know the minute that he saw them together. One step at a time, that's all they could do.

Looking down at her laying snugly under the covers, he knew that he had made the right choice. Having known from the moment that he laid eyes on her that they were meant to be. Maybe deep-down Uncle Sal knew, that's why he insisted that Luc take lead on the case for so many years. That Luc would protect her better than anyone. Removing his shoes and sliding into bed beside her, he would be the comfort she needed. If anyone was after her, they would have to go threw him first.

Waking up from one of the deepest sleeps that Adrianna had had in a long time, she needed a minute to adjust to her surroundings.

Looking beside her, realizing where she was, a calm washed over her. There they were lying under his duvet fully dressed, make-up running down her face and his arm holding her against his chest, knowing she was safe. Slipping out from beneath his arm she headed to the bathroom to freshen up. He looked so peaceful she thought as she gazed down at him. Deep even breathes, his head resting on his arms, hair loosely falling on his face. He had held her in his arms the entire night ensuring her safety, she couldn't help but smile. After freshening up, she slipped back under the covers. Snuggling back up to him.

This was a position that she was beginning to enjoy and could easily get used to. Arching her head up and slowly trailing kisses up his jaw bone, she could begin to feel her center swell. She needed this, needed this release. Needed it for herself. Feeling her against him, her warm breath on his neck, he couldn't ask for a better wake up. More content that she had ever felt, this was what it was supposed to be like. This was what she wanted every morning.

Without even saying a word, taking his time removing their clothes, methodically trailing kisses along her body with each item he discarded. A job he was more than willing to do, give each area of skin the attention it deserved. Lingering leaving hot kisses on her midsection, know the further he went the greater the reward. Sliding his hands up her sides, reaching for the firm high breasts, only covered with the soft satin undergarment, as smile and slow moan escaped his lips. Aching for just a taste, his lips for her aching for his touch. He could feel his mouth watering at the thought while he rubbed her already aching bud, hardening with his touch. Circling it with his tongue, while kneading them at the same time.

Easing himself lower, knowing he would return to finish what he started above, feeling himself needed elsewhere. Her moans and panting guiding him on. Slipping his hand into her panties, already feeling her wetness though the lacey material, damp against his skin. Her moisture bringing him even more pleasure. Ripping them free form her body, his response fleeting with control.

Watching as her legs drifted apart, opening herself to him. Slipping his tongue into her hot velvety folds, lapping and suckling with feverish need. Dipping his tongue deeper into her wetness, savoring her taste on its tip. His finger slipping though the folds while her clit hovered in his mouth. Her need growing as she tightened around his finger. Grinding her hips into his touch wanting more. Sucking hard feeling the orgasm ripping through her body. Wrapping his arms around her, rolling her on top of his body, her soft naked body against his, had him pulsing for more.

Shifting her position, straddling his legs, wanting to bring him just as much pleasure as she received. Trailing her lips from his jaw, nipping his lips, pulling away before he could capture them. Slowly and gently weaving a path down his neck, feeling the shiver that ran down his body. Trailing across his body, feeling the power beneath her touch. Cupping his heavy sack in her hands, while placing the hot wet heat of her mouth across his tip. Gliding her hand over his shaft, while sinking his flesh between her lips, massaging his swollen sack while her lips did all the work.

The slight flicks of her tongue against his swollen tip, taking him deeper, flicking faster with each thrust. He needed to gain control. Shifting their position, wanting to give her as much pleasure once more. Sinking his fingers into her core once more, the heat calling his mouth forward, lapping at her wetness. He'd held back as long as he could. Once she was ready, he wouldn't be able to hold his seed back any longer. Her body pulsing beneath his touch as his seed escaped his body while she swallowed it back. Collapsing on top of one another, ragged breaths through their laboring chests.

"This is one of the most wonderful mornings I have had in a very long time."

"I could say the same thing myself Adrianna. Have you thought about the letter from yesterday, and what you would like to do?"

"Shower first if you'll join me, Then I think that I would like to meet him. I have already lost so much time; I don't want to lose anymore. Can you arrange it for me?" Her heart skipping a beat with anticipation.

"How's later today sound? I can make a call and let you know when."

"Thank you, Luc, I would really appreciate that. I think that I am

134

going to go home quick and clean up. I don't want to meet my father looking like this." She said as she placed a quick kiss on his lips.

"I think that I might get into a bit of trouble from my uncle myself, if he sees you like this too."

"Hang on. Your uncle......my dad...........your boss? All the same person? Oh, my goodness and I was right there, in the building. I was that close to my father and didn't even know it?"

Pushing herself up, as realization began to sit in. So close and she didn't know.

"Adrianna. Hun. He wasn't in the building when you were there, he had left a little while prior to your arrival. Don't worry, everything will be fine."

"When he said that we had been so close, he was only a fifteen-minute drive and I didn't know. How did I not know that he was there? How did my mom not know?"

"Mary was protecting the both of you. You could have been right in front of him, and neither of you would have known. That's how her spell worked. She needed to keep you, and your mother safe because someone was trying to hurt you. It's no one's fault, it just the way it was."

"Maybe, we should see if Mary has talked with your dad first before you see him, just so we are all on the same page. I will arrange for it and then you two can meet later today. Go home and get ready, I will pick you up later and take you to meet your dad."

"Um, Luc. Remember how we got here; do you think that you could...you know

possibly....pop me back home since I don't know how it's done yet?"

"Oh, yea sorry. I forgot about that. Grab your stuff and I will flash you over. I will just give my cousin a quick call to tell her where to go, and she better go now."

A quick call to Mary, and she was on her way to meet uncle Sal. Luc wrapped his arms around Adrianna and before she knew it, she was back in her own apartment.

CHAPTER TEN

Mary knew seeing uncle Sal again, wasn't going to be much fun. She was going to have a

lot of explaining. There was no way of knowing who, Adrianna's parents were. He couldn't

hold her responsible for that. Could he? She just knew, that this poor innocent little witch-ling

needed protection. How could she turn her back, nobody with a soul would? If her uncle didn't understand that then it was his loss.

As far as she was concerned, she protected Adrianna. Kept her safe from the things that went bump in the night. No one would have guessed; the thing was Adrianna's own sister.

Serina was in for one hell of a rude awakening. Mary just wanted front row seats for the show.

"Might as well face the music," Mary muttered to herself. Knowing she could be seen through the glass walls of the office. "Hello uncle Sal, you're looking..." Pausing as she spoke. Seeing the expression on his face, she was more confused than ever.

Relieved that it was Mary that was protecting Adrianna. How she recognized a threat and acted. Understanding, why it was so hard to locate her and her mother.

"My dear Mary, you look as wonderful as you did the last time, I saw you. It's been too long."

"Um, uncle; are you feeling alright?"

Watching as he rose and walked around his desk. He closed the distance between them.

Each step vibrated against the hard floor. Each foot taking an eternity to contact the ground. Her apprehension, as did her confusion grow.
"Yes, Mary I am...At first, when Luc told me, I was furious beyond belief. After some consideration, I owe you a debt of thanks. If it wasn't for you...I don't know what might have

happened."

"I was just working at the right place at the right time. I knew that something was wrong with

the whole situation." Sensing his inner turmoil, he looked like he was beating himself up.
"Sal, what's going on? You seem...I don't know...I just assumed that you would be pissed at

me...want to kill me for what I did or something along those lines."

His eyes sliding closed, the air slowly leaving his lungs. Allowing the cooling effect to ease the tension from his body. As if turning back time in his head, digging up a memory from long ago.
"Adrianna's mom didn't return home for a reason that day. Eventually, I will find out why. But,

you took it upon yourself to protect her. Why did you protect her? How did you know that

something was wrong?"

A look of longing was deep in Sal's eyes. Mary held the answers he needed. After all the years lost with unknowing. He was the closest he had ever been to discovering the truth about the night so long ago.

Thinking back to the night, etched in her memory. Of the young woman, who stumbled into the maternity ward. Confusion surrounded her, unable to answer the simplest of questions.
Recalling the energy that radiated once she took hold of her arm. There had been magic at work.
Panic in her voice, more than just worry of pregnancy. Hesitantly looking around as if trying to determine who she could trust. Catching hold of Mary's gaze, the woman's tension eased. After Adrianna's birth, Mary knew that she had to protect the child. No matter the cost.

Figuring that whoever had put the spell on her mother, didn't want her found. Considered that when they did the spell, they didn't know about the child. They wanted her mother out of the way. Watching and shadowing them for years, but no one ever turned up. Until I moved in next door, making things a lot easier.

His expression didn't change. Taking time to absorb the story. More questions than answers were coming to his mind. Thankful to his niece for helping in all the years he was powerless to. He had hoped the story would fill the hole in his heart. Only causing it to splitter further at the thought of someone out there trying to harm his family. "Mary, who do you think is after Adrianna, and her mother most of all? I know that her mother
is gone, but I just can't accept that."

"I was there when she went passed away. I had the same feeling that something wasn't right. And, to who do I think was after them? I am not sure. The only person that ever had a beef with her mother was Serina. I think she lost it."

"Serina never knew about Adrianna though. I never told her, or Sebastian about the pregnancy."

"That still doesn't mean that she didn't want her out of the picture. And FYI, Serina is back. She

doesn't know me, but I made sure that she knew to stay away."

Seeing the fires light in the depths of Sal's eyes. Never considering that it was Serina who had caused all the trouble. He knew that his daughter resented him, but to hurt someone innocent. He didn't want to imagine what would have happened if she knew that Nina was pregnant.

"What do you mean she is back? Where did you see her?"

"At Adrianna's house. But she wasn't there for her; I think that she was following Luc. The best part about my mother keeping me sequestered away from the family, was that Serina never knew who I was. She still doesn't till this day."

"Why would she follow Luc? She looked after him like a brother when his parents disappeared. She anticipated his every need and helped him with everything. I know she was hurt when he became immortal and needed to find himself but to follow him?"

"That's the whole problem. With Luc and Adrianna together, it won't take long for Serina to figure out who and what she is."

"We just have to make sure that Serina never finds out that Adrianna is her sister."

Pacing the room, Sal needed more answers than Mary could give him. Looking to her for support and help, he knows that she would willingly help as she had throughout the years.

"I will do my best to monitor the situation, but I think that Luc has it well under control, but we

will both work together uncle."

"Thank you, Mary. We just need to put the puzzle together and find the missing piece. It will

turn up soon, I am sure of that."

"I will let you know if anything new happens. I will talk to you later."

"And Mary, take this in thanks for everything that you have done."

After handing the item to Mary, Sal vanished. Looking down into the palm of her hand was her mother's black onyx ring, it was believed to be lost years ago. But how did? How?

"Some things are just better left unknown." She muttered to herself.

Clutching the ring in her hand, she was happy to have part of her mother with her again. Even though her mother wasn't far away, Mary was glad to have a piece of her with her now. Her mother had always given her strength when she needed it. If now wasn't the time, Mary doubted that there ever would be. Slipping the ring onto her index figure, it felt good. Her mother had been so busy with her sister since Sebastian vanished, she almost felt left out. She just hoped that the ring would lead her in the right direction.

Turning it around her finger and made sure that it was sung. Mary knew what needed to be done. Leaving the office, she headed to her condo, she needed to think.

CHAPTER ELEVEN

Watching, from across the street, Serina noticed movement inside the house. Looking closer, realizing what she was seeing, she could feel her blood boiling through her veins. People didn't cross her without consequences; this was going to stop.

"After he leaves, the bitch is mine. Since she knows what we are, she is either one of us or

things around here are more serious than I thought." She said through clenched teeth, anger radiating from her body, the energy in the air charging with her mood.

Knowing her time to act was going to be soon, she needed to devise a plan. Once the bitch was out of the picture, things were going to be a hell of a lot easier for her and Luc to be together. He can't stay much longer; he was going to have to go see her father for their daily meeting soon enough. Once he goes, then the fun will begin Serina thought, and she was looking forward to every minute of it. A sly smile crossed her face, thinking of everything she'd like to do.

Too bad she couldn't say the same for the other woman. At least she had an outlet for all her anger. She didn't need Luc to see her in this state. She would like to be calm when she meets him. Watching as Luc flashed from the house Serina had to act quickly, not knowing how long he would be gone for. Shifting into her best business suit and her most pleasant demeanor. Serina knew what she was going to do as she walked up, and rang the doorbell. The timing was perfect, she couldn't ask for a better chance than right now. Taking a deep breath, she had to focus.

If the person was a witch on the other side, the less she could read from Serina the better.

Putting her walls firmly in place, with a smug smile and a gleam in her eyes, there would be no stopping her. Ring the bell she used all her control just to not blow the door open. She couldn't afford to blow it, not when she was so close.

"One second, I will be right there."

"Hello, may I help you?"

"Yes, hello. My name is Miss Rina, I am going around asking for donations for the local charities. We are selling antique picture frames with all the proceeds going to help. Can I show you a few of them, to see if any interest you?"

"Um, I am actually on my way out. Do you have a brochure or something that I can order from?"

"No, sorry we just have the samples that we carry with us. It will only take but a minute."

Come on let me in the house already, I don't have all day, Luc could pop back in any minute, she thought as she looked the girl squarely in the eyes.

"If it will only take a minute, I have a very important meeting to get to." With a twist in her gut, she hesitantly let the saleswoman in.

"Thank you so much," Serina said with a smirk.

"This way, you can show me in the living room. You said antique frames?"

"Yes, they were all donated by a founding family, who just wants to help in the area. I have one here, that I think will be something, that you would definitely look good in." She tried to hide the irony in her voice.

"Sounds good let me get my wallet while you get it out." With all her alarm bells going off, she wished Luc had taught her that vanishing trick earlier.

"I have this one that would look great with your decor. Have a look, see what you think."

Before Adrianna could do or say anything else, it was like she was frozen, unable to move or speak. All she remembered was a purple haze surrounding her and that laugh, that laugh that she would not soon forget. She was in trouble, hoping that someone would could help her. Peering out she could see her room, and then slowly everything began to vanish, and the dread in her began to rise.

\#   \#   \#

"Luc, what time did you tell Adrianna to meet us?" Sal was beginning to get anxious, "Maybe it
was just too much for her in one day." Finding himself, as edgy as a child waiting for their friend to arrive. Glancing repeatedly at his watch, Luc's trepidation was growing.

"Something isn't right Uncle; I can feel it! I know it! Can't place it. You don't think?"

With a sharp pain in his heart, grabbing his chest Luc felt his world torn apart. Never, had he experienced such pain in his life. As if his heart was being ripped from his body, his ribs splintering from the pain. Looking up at his uncle, knowing by the look in his eyes, the fire that was simmering below the surface was now at full rage. He could deal with Sal's anger later, right now she needed him. Her panic kicking his into hyperdrive; she needed help. Looking at his uncle, his world once again would be torn apart.

"Someone has Adrianna, I think Serina found her."

"No! I just got her back, when I get my hands on the insufferable daughter of mine, she will

pay."

Like an explosion, the glass walls in the office began to vibrate with the energy. The cracks projecting outwards like ripples in a lake. With the emotions, Sal was radiating everything was being strained.

"I am going to get Mary; we need all the help that we can get."

Luc had to find Mary, and fast! If Serina did have Adrianna, she would be in serious trouble. He just hoped that Ad would think quickly on her feet and put two and two together. Luc knew that he was going to need more than just Mary's help. Things were going to get ugly. He needed her safe and out of Serina's hands; there was no telling what she was capable of.

#   #   #

Engulfed in a haze of smoke; her vision impaired as she could feel her body growing tighter. Each gasp for air felt like acid burning through her. Unable to move, her limbs felt like stone. The weight unbearable under the pressure. Straining to move even the smallest of muscles, to gain some feeling of control.

As quickly as the haze came over her it was gone. Cool air filling her lungs once more,
the tension and weight leaving her body. Regaining control, a heat filling her core wanting to protect her from any further harm.
"Let me out of here! Who the hell are you and what do you want with me?"
"It won't do any good darling, yelling at her like that. You're not going to get out. Trust us we have been here for centuries." Hearing someone shout at her, Adrianna just couldn't figure out from where.
"For what? You have got to be kidding me! No way in hell I am hanging out in this place for that long. I just got my life and I am not going to let her have it." Searching for something to aid her, but only finding emptiness around her.

Staring into the frame, knowing there was no hope for escape. Serina took pleasure in watching the girl struggle.
"Would you shut the hell up! Luc is mine and you will never see him again. I thought you were just a client, so I was patient. Then I

realized that you weren't. I have worked hard to ensure he is mine, and some whore isn't going to take him from me."

"Tramp, who the hell are you to call me a tramp? I don't even know who you are, you

egotistical, conniving, selfish bitch."

If Mary had ever taught her anything it was to speak her mind. Unfortunately, now probably wasn't the best time for her verbal filter to fall off.

Relishing in her latest prizes' agony. Nothing made her happier. Leaning forward, to allow her captive to get a better look. A gleam in her eyes. Letting the rant continue for her own amusements. Reaching for a cloth to polish the glass in the frame, just to show how little power the girl had.

"I am Serina you bitch, and don't you forget it! Who the hell are you?"

"Holly....my name is Holly."

If she knew who I was, she would kill me. The less she knows, the better. No wonder our father never told her about me. Was this who was causing all my problems from the beginning? A conniving older sister. Good thing I was quick on her feet.

"Well Holly, I hope that you like your new little home because you will be there for a very long time. And if I were you; I wouldn't worry about Luc finding you, because he never will. Just ask his parents, they have been with me for years."

Taking the frame from the other shelf, she moved it so that the two could face each other then she disappeared. Staring into the frame, Adrianna knew that her sister would stop at nothing to get what she wanted. Lucky for Adrianna, they just may have been cut from the same cloth.

Ad was just glad she met. Luc when she did. If it wasn't for him bringing her back to her normal self, she would still be the shy depressed girl hiding from the world. He ignited just enough of a fire in her, and she'd use it to her advantage.

Luc's parents were still alive? That couldn't be right. They had been lost so many centuries ago. Serina couldn't have kept them trapped for that long. This woman was evil; she would have to be careful. More lives than just hers were on the line. Looking around and taking stock in her surroundings. Adrianna realized that she was looking out. Serina must have trapped her in the frame.
'So much for an antique, try cursed. That bitch.' She looked out and seeing rows and rows of frames. She could not know how many people were trapped inside. This wasn't right. She couldn't play with people's lives. All those children; parents wondering where their loved ones were. How could someone be so cruel? Taking a deep breath and trying to focus, there had to be something she could do.

She needed to keep her identity to herself. If Serina found out that she was her sister, things were going to go from bad to shear hell. At least Serina had left, but who knows for how long? Mary had done such a great job at hiding her. Perhaps she should have been training her on how to get out of this situation. She could have learned how not to get herself captured. Adrianna couldn't fault Mary; she only did what she felt was right.

"Excuse me. EXCUSE ME."

"We are trapped, not deaf honey, we can hear you."

"Sorry. How long will she be gone for?"

"An hour. A day. A week. A century. Who knows with that one, she comes and goes, only to

make sure that nobody discovers what she is up to."

"She said that you are Luc's parents, is that true?" Seeing that the name meant something to the

woman, Adrianna knew that she was right.

At hearing her son's name, Christina began to cry. For centuries, she wanted to know what happened to Luc. Just once, she wanted someone to know him. All the years that she had been trapped, her only regret was not spending more time. Christina missed her sons' youth. Missed them growing up and for that, she would never forgive herself. She and Charles had to go away for the weekend to protect Luc from getting hurt.

She was pregnant, and they chose to hide the pregnancy from him, in case anything happened. He had had such a hard time, and Charles almost lost Luc and Christina when he was born and didn't want Luc to go through the pain in case his sibling didn't survive.

At least he was safe. The family they had left Matteo with, would love and look after him, not knowing that they didn't have a choice. They just went for a walk and never came back. The family knowing, they would never do something like that. Leaving him with a dear friend who would protect their new baby with their lives. Hopefully one day their children would meet, and they would. With this new woman here, Christina and Charles had renewed hope. A child that neither of them ever had a chance to see mature, a part of their life that was taken away from them. At least Serina didn't know about Matteo. He was still safely hidden.

"You know my son. You know Luc?" With hope and anticipation, Christina had to know.

"Yes, you could say we are kind of together or were until crazy lady here trapped me. You have no idea when she will be back? There has to be a way out of this thing." Distracted by trying to escape, Adrianna wasn't really paying attention to the questions being asked.

"Please tell us, is Luc alright? Is he happy? Is he as handsome as we remember him?"

It didn't even dawn on Ad that they must have been sick with worry, not knowing how their son had faired. She felt like an insensitive fool.

"I am so sorry; I didn't mean to. It's just that. Yes, Yes, he is a wonderful handsome man who I

care a great deal for. He is well educated, and his uncle Sal has taken very good care of him.

They searched for you for years, but nothing ever came of it. He is a lawyer and works with Sal still, that's how we met." Adrianna could see the relief in their eyes, she couldn't give much information, but we're grateful for what she knew.

"Thank you. Just to know that he is alright and happy, I can be at peace. All these years we have been stuck here, thinking every day about our boys. It's our own form of torture."

"Boys? I thought Luc was an only child. He never said anything about a brother."

"That's because he didn't know. The weekend we left him with Sal, it was because we were going to have our second child. Serina doesn't know so please don't say anything to her. She would stop at nothing to find him and trap him just to hurt us more."

"I won't, I promise. But why are you here? How did this happen?"

So many more questions were coming to her. Like pieces to a puzzle that would all fit together, she was sure of it. A person wouldn't go this far, trapping all the people that Luc loved for no reason at all. "Serina wanted Luc for herself, even when he was little. She was determined that they were to be together. He looked at her like a sister. She thought that if she had him all to herself, that as he aged, she could change his feeling towards her. She decided that if we weren't in the picture so to speak, that she would have control over him and guide him.

We ran into her on our walk, and she wanted to show us what she had bought at the shops. We didn't question what she was doing so far from home. One minute she showed us the frame, and the next thing that we knew we were trapped. We can talk to the other people, but no one has found a way out."

"So, she trapped you in here to keep Luc to herself? She's crazy, completely crazy. How many

people, do you think there are in this room?"

"It's hard to say. People usually come and go quickly because they give her what she wants. But for us, she leaves us here so that we can't tell him the truth. We are just glad to hear that she didn't influence him."

"Well, I can tell you he thinks that she is nuts and would do anything to keep her out of his life.

She has been away from him for a long time, so why now? Why would she want this?

Now? I don't get it."

"I think that she has a bigger plan. Two other women and we have been here the longest. One is her father's coven's elder and very powerful. But her body weakens, and she is unable to escape. Serina injured her before trapping her. She doesn't heal and has been in pain for a century. The other is very feisty and keeps goading her. She isn't like us; we aren't sure what she is."

Christina hoped that one day, the woman would find the peace that she was looking for.

She doesn't like to see the woman suffer.

"Thank you so much for telling me your story. I am going to find a way out. There must be a way out. Luc will find us I know it."

"He can't, the whole place is charmed. There is no way, that's why she took us together. She

knew if she separated us, she wouldn't win."

Adrianna knew deep down Luc would find her. They were connected, and she could feel it. When she didn't show up for the meeting with her father, he would know something was wrong. He would find her, he had to. She didn't promise him forever just to lose him now. The realization began to set in on the meaning of the words. She would deal with that if she ever got out.

"Excuse me, what is your name, you never told us?"

"It's Holly, you can call me Holly." Adrianna didn't want to put them into more trouble than they already were in. "Are you sure that there isn't a way out, like a back door, a loophole, or

something?" Thinking of everything she'd ever learned about magic from movies. There was always a way out of a spell, there had to be.

"We tried for years and found nothing, but our power weakens each year that we are here.

Serina's spells are strong, like nothing that I have ever seen. Only a member of her family with as much power as hers could break it. She would never imprison one of them unless they

were weakened already, even she isn't that stupid."

They might not have thought so, but Adrianna knew better. Serina did trap a member of her family, she just didn't know it. Only if she had her full power. Who was she kidding?

She wouldn't even know what to do with any of it. She was never trained. Sal said that they trained since childhood so they could control their abilities. This was going to be hopeless she thought to herself. There had to be something; something was missing. What was it though?

Adrianna wasn't going down without a fight. One day, with enough practice, Serina was going to kiss her sorry ass goodbye. Adrianna had all the time in the world to practice. What she was going to practice? She had no idea. But, was sure that something would come to her. As a child, she was always told that you crawl before you walk, walk before you run, and run when you got into trouble and fast. She would crawl. Let's just see what kind of witch she can be.
"Christina, Charles. We are going to get out of here and that I am promising you. Before you
know it we will be free and Serina won't even know what hit her!" Adrianna said confidently, she had her own secrets.

She just got her life back and wasn't going to go down without a fight. Serina wanted Luc, that wasn't going to happen if she could do anything about it. Her dear sister was going to get more than she bargained for. Underestimating Adrianna was the first flaw in her plan.

AWAKEN THE FLAMES

CHAPTER TWELVE

Luc knew the second that something happened to Adrianna. His heart began to tighten, and he couldn't breathe. He couldn't figure out what. Feeling her panic and he couldn't do a damn thing about it. It was driving him mad. He needed to focus so that they could find her. "Luc, come on talk to us," Mary pleaded. She was almost glad that Luc made Adrianna promise forever with him. At least now they had a chance.

"She's scared, I can feel it. I can feel her every emotion. She is confused and confined somehow. I can feel her checking out her surroundings. This isn't right, why would Serina do this? How did she get to her? You still had her protected didn't you Mary?" Panic setting in, feeling his pulse racing. He had to find her; he was going to find her.

"Of course, she was protected. But I don't think that Serina realizes who she has."

Looking over at Sal, they both had the same questions. How had she gotten Adrianna? And what was she up to?

"Luc, we will find her. I promise." Mary's heart went out to her cousin; hoping that one day

she'd have someone who cared as much for her.

"Do you mind telling me; how in the hell you know that my daughter is missing Luc? You know what? Don't tell me. But I am glad it was you over anyone else."

157

Relieved that at least they might have a chance of finding Adrianna. He would deal with
the fact that his nephew was now his son-in-law later.

Calling in all their resources. They had to do whatever they could to locate Serina. If she
figured out who she was, Adrianna was going to be in a lot more trouble than she was already in.

"Luc, I don't think that Serina knows who Adrianna is. I think that they are using her to hurt
you." Realizing the words as she spoke them, Mary knew what was going on.

"Would you like to explain that again? Why would she want to do that?"

"Luc think about it. She has enough power to get past my magic, and get to her without knowing who she really is? Serina wants you for her prize so that no one else could, have you? It's not that hard to figure out. You are the only one who can find Adrianna and I need you to concentrate? Serina isn't trying to hurt you. She just wants you. For herself."

"No, she couldn't. I made it clear centuries ago. She's not that stupid? If she finds out, shit, Adrianna is going to need help fast. I am going to kill Serina when I find her." Knowing what kind of person Serina really was, Luc had to act fast.

"That's the problem, Luc, no one knows where to find her. She has been gone, hidden for years. For her to know about Adrianna, she

158

would have to know where you have been in the last two months. Serina would have had to been following you."

"I knew that I was being watched. I just thought it was my nerves from being around Adrianna.

But Serina was there the entire time."

Not wanting to show Mary and Sal how truly scared he was. Guessing that his reaction gave it away. Luc had to come up with something. Serina was going to wish that she'd stayed hidden and stayed gone forever. They had no future; he could never be with such a person. Adrianna was his love, his life. He needed to find her, needed to save her and have her with him. He could do this, they were connected. It wasn't going to be a strong connection. The timing was too short, but he could do it.

Rubbing the spot on his chest, knowing that it was the only key to her feelings and safety. 'I am going to get you, Adrianna, no matter what, I will find you' he thought to himself.

He could feel her emotions rising, his blood pumped faster with anticipation. She was a

fighter. Afraid she would try something that would get herself hurt if she wasn't careful. He knew, Adrianna wasn't going to go down just because Serina wanted her too. He just prayed that

Ad didn't say anything to draw more attention to herself before they could get to her.

Not only did they have to find Adrianna; but they couldn't let Serina know what they were up to. If she found out, innocent people

159

would be put at risk. He couldn't live with himself if that happened. Ad's safety was priority one, she had to stay protected.

His best friends growing up Paul and Vincent were going to be his biggest support.

They had a long-time beef with Serina, one that needed to be settled. The three of them together, were unstoppable. Once the boys realized what was at stake, there was no going back. They always stuck together no matter what. This time wasn't going to be any different.

Neither Paul nor Vince had found their partners yet. They viewed Luc as their brother, when you messed with one, you dealt the wrath of all three. Watching as his friends appeared before him, he knew it wouldn't take them long. With their skills combined, they were unstoppable.

"Luc, you said she was following you, why don't we retrace your steps over the last few weeks."

"We have already done that Paul, but it turned up nothing. It's like she doesn't exist. We have been everywhere and nothing."

"Have you rechecked Adrianna's place? Maybe something was left behind" Vincent was convinced that they were missing something.

"Mary is over there right now checking things out. Let me message her first before we go over, so, we don't startle her."

"Mary? Who's Mary?"

"Mary, my cousin. Who was protecting Adrianna all these years? It's a long story and I will fill
you in later."

Sending a quick message; Luc, Paul, and Vince flashed over to Adrianna's house. There had to be a piece of information, somewhere in Ad's house. If Serina was at the point of no return, she would start to get sloppy, she always did when she got excited.

Arriving they ripped the place apart. The rooms, everything. Adrianna wasn't going to like the mess when she came home. As long as she came home, none of them cared. They went over everything again and still nothing. His frustrations mounted. There had to be something they were missing.

Mary knew that something wasn't right, but she couldn't see it. She had found her wallet in the middle of the floor. All her cards, and money spilling out. Trying to focus and find anything that could help them. It had happened in the family room. It was quick. She could see that there wasn't a struggle. It was too easy. Ad didn't even put up a fight. Why hadn't she put up a fight? Adrianna never would have gone willingly. She was always a scrapper growing up. Fighting for what she believed in. So why now? Why not fight? It just didn't make sense.

She must have trusted Serina, not knowing who she was. The door was unlocked and there were no traces of magic on it. Adrianna must have let her in. But why? What was Serina offering her? What did she give her? Mary was getting more questions than answers.

"Can any of you come up with anything? Luc? Something? Anything at all."

"Mary, I got nothing. Vincent, do you remember when we were kids, and we played hide and go seek? How did you always find us? You never told us how you just did."

"I tracked you. It was easy when I am homed into your signature, I can trace you. It's just what
I do. But I haven't met Adrianna, and I don't know her signature. I can't track her unless I
have a connection to her in some form or another."

Vince really wished he could help his friend, but the dead end was driving him crazy. It didn't help that Mary was helping them look for her, there was something about her. It was distracting. He had to concentrate on Adrianna though, Mary, he could deal with that later. Whatever was drawing him to her was strong, leaving him at a loss. He never had a feeling like this before; he was going to sort it out. That was going to be on his to-do list.

Getting more agitated by the minute and not being able to help, Paul decided to start cleaning up the mess that they had made. Maybe in the mists of all the chaos, they missed something crucial. Starting in the family room, he organized her pictures and her belongings back to their original places. He had a knack of knowing where something belonged just by touching it. Noticing the bag under the table he picked it up. Right away he knew where to start looking, and no one was going to like it.

"Hey, guy's over here. It's a bag from The Gilded Mirror, have you heard of it?" As they looked around, it took them a few minutes to put the pieces together. It was a craft store that their elders dealt with. But, why would she go there?

"She didn't. Someone else did. I think that we should pay the store a visit."

Agreeing that the store was their priority. The owner wasn't getting away without answering a few questions first. That they would all make sure of it. The store was cluttered, that Luc didn't think they would ever find the person that worked there. Frames, mirrors, statues, pendants, the place was filled with relics. Some so old he couldn't date. Feeling the presence of powerful magic. Where Adrianna was concerned, he didn't care what he had to face. Whatever had to be done to get her back safe would he do.

Someone was watching him and Paul, they could feel it, but it wasn't Serina. Paul was getting nervous, he hated being spied on. Whoever was here was taking their time. Which wasn't something that they had an abundance of now. Luc became more uneasy as the clock slowly counted the seconds as they passed. This was taking way too long.

Mary was protecting them; Luc could feel her magic. Hoping that it was enough. So many things could go wrong, he just hoped that nothing did. Reaching out with his senses, knowing that Adrianna hadn't been harmed. She was confused. His heart ached for her, unsure what she was facing. He had to get to her soon.

"May I help you with something?" called a frail voice from the distance.

"Yes. My boss sent me here to purchase a frame; he was looking for something to go in his

office."

"Well sir, we sell many frames. For what purpose are you acquiring one for, so I can help you in

that direction."

"He has quite a few adversaries, that would mean to harm him and those he cares about. Not

wanting to do anything drastic, but would like them to learn their lesson for a short period of time."

"Well, were you looking for something for confusion, imprisonment or grief? We have a very

wide selection."

Just the thought of someone being this cold-hearted. He knew that Serina was capable of it, but for there to be this high of a demand. Something wasn't right in the universe. There was an unnatural balance to things? Good and evil weren't aligned now, and it would take Luc, Adrianna, Sal and everyone else to help put it back to normal. Thinking of something that the sisters said a few years ago. Something big was going to happen; Luc just hoped that his side would win in the end.

"Possibly one of each, you know that you can never be unprepared."
Who was this man? Luc was sure that he knew him? He wasn't a warlock, but he obviously knew of their world.
"Right this way. These have been very popular in the last few years."

There in front of Luc and Paul were rows of frames. They looked harmless enough to the naked eye. But once you gazed deeper into it you could see there was a whole other realm. The shopkeeper continued to inform them that once you placed your person inside the frame, they would remain there for as long as you wanted. There really was no way out. There were only a few accounts of people escaping them, but they had an incredible amount of power.

Thanking the man for his time and informing him that he would return with his boss to make the purchase, they just wanted to get out. Filling Mary and Vince in on the details, they all agreed that they had to work fast to find Adrianna. Knowing what was used to trap her, they just needed to find her and get her out.
"Luc, is she alright? I know that you can sense her."

Mary wasn't only concerned for Adrianna, but her cousin as well. She knew what this could do to him, she had watched her sister search for years almost to the point of madness looking for Sebastian. Babbling that he was right there with them. That he was always watching over her. Her obsession over the beach house and refusal to leave it. Just sitting on the shore watching as the waves broke and the changing of the tides. She didn't want Luc to be lost like

Elena. Mary's family was riddled with curses, she hoped he wasn't the next victim.

"She is crying, and I am not there to comfort her. But something else, I can't place what it is;

almost like confusions but happiness at the same time."

"She is strong Luc, more than you realize. I think more than any of us really understand."

Needing more information, they flashed back to Sal's. Sal would have to call in some favors to help find his daughter. Luc knew that it wasn't going to be an issue. He just hoped that the old woman was willing to help. She was more stubborn than Sal.

He knew that Sal hated talking to her, but he really didn't have much of a choice at this point. Here's hoping that she is in a good mood when she gets the call.

CHAPTER THIRTEEN

Looking around, realizing that there wasn't much to work with, Adrianna had to focus. Her anger burned like fire coursing through her veins The more she thought about what her friends were going through; the more frustrated she became. Her emotions building, feeling them trying to take over.

The energy consuming her. A burning need for release radiated through her body. Looking down a red cast covered over her hands, she could see a red cast over them. They were burning, but she felt no pain. Startled and shocked, with a quick flip of her hand, the fire was gone. How had she done that? What was going on? She didn't know if she should ask Christina and Charles, the less that they knew, the better; for now. Needing their help would come soon enough; but first, she needed to figure herself out. What was she?

She could feel the power mount with her emotions. Could feel the energy radiating over her body. Hell, her hands were just on fire. How the hell did that happen? Time would tell. But whatever she could do, she needed control of it first.

There had to be something, her father mentioned in the letter that she was meant to do something great. That she would have a power like no other, but what was it? If only she could see her mother again and ask her for the truth. Why had she lied all those years? There was just so much that she didn't understand her world was crashing down around her.

Years of emotions, trapped. She thought she expressed them when she told Luc. There was more buried under the surface. Maybe they held the answers? Could there be something she had forgotten? Some lessons long lost? Slipping her eyes closed in hopes that it would pull something to the surface. As if in a dream, Adrianna, she could feel things dissolving, fading away. What was happening? What was going on? Before she knew it, Adrianna was there in the room facing her mother.

But how? It must have been a dream? Blinking back the tears from her eyes, so she could see through the haze, overrun by emotions. Her chest constricting making it hard to breathe, while her heart rate increased. Feeling overpowered, this couldn't be happening. How could her mother be standing there, in front of her like it was yesterday?

Reaching her hand forward, ever so slightly pulling back. Afraid to touch, to make actual contact, not wanting the image in front of her to fade away. It was too real. If she had learned anything in the last few weeks, it was that anything was possible. Having her mother before she

wasn't something she had ever considered. But now...

"Mom? Is that you?" Trying to remain calm as the blackness threaten her. Needing answers and now was not the time to pass out. Feeling

168

the fire beginning to burn deep within her pushing the darkness aside, realizing it was the warmth needed to regain her focus.

"Yes Adrianna, it is, and I am glad that you came."

More confused than ever, this couldn't be happening. Slowly with an unsteady hand,

Adrianna reached out further. As they touched, she could feel the warmth of her mother's skin.

"Mom? How? What? Are you?" Tears streaming down her cheeks, happiness burning through.

Adrianna had her mother in her arms, and would fight to keep her.

"Yes, darling it's me, but you only have a moment. I know that you don't understand but you will, just concentrate and it will be fine. I am sorry for keeping the truth from you all those years, but you needed to be safe. Your father didn't even realize what I was. I didn't want to leave him; I didn't know what came over me. It took me years to figure it out. Then when I finally realized what Mary was, I was grateful. I knew that she was protecting us. I never told her who or what I really was. The less that the two of you knew, the better. We will see each other again, for that I am certain. Just think of me when you need me, and you will come."

"Mom, I don't understand? Mom! Mom!" Before Adrianna knew what was happening, the world around her was going out of focus once again, and finding herself back in the frame.

Not knowing what else to do, Adrianna was more confused than ever. It was her mother the day before she passed away, she knew it.

Breaking down and began to cry and refused to stop until all her tears were done. Having felt her mother warmth, her touch, only for it to be ripped from her again. The feeling of led came rushing back.

What had her mother meant when she said keeping the truth from her? And not telling

Mary who she really was? Her life was just getting stranger by the minute. But, one thing as certain. She was coming into her powers, whatever they were. Once she figured them out;

Serina was going to be in more trouble than she would know.

"Honey, don't cry. There is nothing that you can do. Until Serina decides that you aren't a

threat to Luc and her, she isn't going to let you go." Christina just wanted to comfort her but knew that nothing was really going to help, Adrianna had looked so distraught her heart went

out to her.

"It's just so much. I just found my father, met Luc and my life was finally getting back on track,

and that woman traps me. She doesn't even know me. All because she wanted Luc? "

Adrianna wanted to tell them so much more, but their lives would be in even more trouble. She was glad that she had Christina to talk to though. If she couldn't have her own mother, she at least knew that Luc's would be more than willing to listen.

"Holly, just relax. Maybe if Serina thinks that you and Luc are finished, she would let you go.

170

You need to convince her."

"Luc is going to find me, that I can promise you. When he does, you will be free too. You,

Charles, the old woman, and whoever else she has trapped in this hell hole. Serina picked the wrong person to deal with this time."

Feeling the power building in her, she needed to be in controlled. Unfortunately, at that moment, she didn't have any control of her emotions. She could feel the flames licking her arms and just hoped no one noticed.

"The other lady that's here, she isn't like us. I know what you are but Serina doesn't. I can sense the power in people. But her, I can't figure it out. She has definite power, but she isn't a witch. She tries to escape but curses every time when it doesn't work.

I just wish that my words comforted her, instead they just push her that much more over the edge. She refuses to tell us who or what she is. Just mumbles something about a secret that needs to come out. The poor thing." Christina's heart went out to the woman, whoever she was.

One day if they ever escaped, she would help her with her quest, no matter what it is.

"And the old woman. You said that Serina injured her before she trapped her. Why?"

"She is very powerful. But because she can't heal from her injuries while trapped, she is slowly

aging and her powers are fading. If she can ever get free, Serina would never see the light of
day."

"What are her powers, Christina? Do you think that she will ever be free?"

"For what her powers are that I can't tell you. I just know that she is the root of all good in our world. Her power is unparalleled; her descendent have only a fraction of what she has. Even in her weakened state she is still a threat to Serina's plans. And yes, one day she will be free."

Adrianna wished she could see the old woman, and have her know that there was hope.
She would find it; needing to concentrate and strengthen herself. Whatever she did earlier, she needed to do again. How was the million-dollar question, but she would. For her, Christina, Charles, the old women, and the other woman, she would get them out. Even if it took centuries, she wasn't going down without a fight.

Knowing that she wouldn't wait for others to free her, that just wasn't in her but a little help would be welcomed. Her mother always told her she knew how to cause trouble, and how to get out of it. This one time that she was hoping that her mother was right. Mary had told her that if she could concentrate, she would be able to achieve something great. Hoping that something great was going to happen soon, after the last forty-eight hours with Luc, waiting wasn't her strong point.

Knowing that it was late, Adrianna looked over to make sure that everyone was asleep. She didn't need them to see her trying that again. But whatever it was she did earlier, she just hoped that she could do it again. Concentrating on the palm of her hand and willing herself, just thinking of fire, and nothing. Her frustration was growing.

'How did I do it the first time? I was so mad.' Trying to get mad again, which truly wasn't that hard of a thing to do, she still got nothing.

'Fire, come on fire. You can do it come to me........ARRRRG' something else, what else?

Sitting there and thinking, maybe something would trigger it. 'Just relax Ad, you can do this.

All these people are counting on you.' She muttered.

Maybe she was going about it all wrong, had to be an easier way. She just needed to sit back and relax, knowing full well that she could do it. Letting all her emotions wash over her, she could feel the palm of her hand begin to warm up. The love she had for her family, her mom, dad, Luc, and Mary there had to be a key. How they must be worrying about her, not knowing what happened.

Her hand started to glow, and she could see the flames taking the shape of her profile. Each of her fingers, the palm of her hand, it radiated up her arm and across her chest. Through her body fire radiated all around, like a surge of power. She could control fire, it covered every inch of her, like a second skin. With each of her movements, it gracefully flowed. Loving astrology and knowing about it, she never even considered that her birth would truly affect her outcome. She was an Aries, the ram, the first cardinal symbol, Fire. Pure, unadulterated fire. The energy shot through her body like nothing she had ever felt, controlling the element. Now it was beginning to make sense.

When she was a child and reached for the stove and touched the burner by accident;
she didn't get burned; she was energized. Her mother never scolded her, just stared at her in amazement. Maybe mom knew that she was different? But why hadn't she said anything? Why did she keep it all to herself? Adrianna just wanted to know, why did her mother do what she did? And for once, Ad could ask her. 'Just concentrate Ad, you can do it. Think back to that
day in the kitchen.' And slowly, things began to dissolve, and Adrianna was back in her home, just many years earlier.
"Mom, mom, is that you?"

Afraid of it being a dream not wanting it to be, she had to guard her emotions. She could see the woman standing over a soapy sink, cleaning the dishes. Her hair flowing over her shoulders, humming to herself, seeming to be lost in the moment. The faint smell of green apples in the air, with cinnamon and honey hovering in the background. Taking the moment to live in the memory in front of her, and bookmark it in her mind.

The aromas filling the room, all she could do was enjoy the moment. This was what home was, not what she had condemned herself to live over the last year. When the woman turned to face her, the expression was one Ad would never soon forget.

"Adrianna" rushing to give her daughter a hug, knowing that their time together wouldn't last long. "Adrianna, I am so happy to see you all grown up, I am glad you learned how to travel."

Embracing her mother and letting all the familiarity wash over her. She needed this hug, more then she needed anything else. This was one of the things she missed most about having her mother around.

"Mom, why didn't you ever tell me? There are so many questions that I need to be answered. How is this possible, how is any of it possible?"

"What do you mean I never told you? I told you the stories ever since the day you were born.

Do you not recall them?"

"Stories, the ones you told me at bedtime? I thought nothing of them. Just a way for you to put me to sleep. You were always one for the dramatics." She started smiling at the details her

mother was reminding her of.

"Those stories were of our history, your history. You are a very special child. Your future is bright and shining. Not many people have your ability. Why do you think me and my brother never got along? Because my brother wanted revenge, his ability was taken from him and he wanted to use you. That's why I kept the two of you apart, for your safety."

175

Hoping that Ad would remember all the stories from her youth, they were the key to her power. And why didn't she know about it, what was going on in the future? She needed to remember. But with all the stress going on now, she wasn't sure if she would be able to. "Can you tell me anything else, what other things that I can do? I need to know everything."

There were so many things going through her mind, she didn't know where to start. "Nothing that I can think of off hand, we can only jump through time. But don't try and fix anything big, just small things. You could do too much. You could change more than just your own history. Your father never knew what I could do, he wouldn't have understood. There was just so many things to consider. He kept pushing for us to be together, but he would never be able to accept what I could do. There were too many secrets, too much for a mortal to understand." "Mortal, what do you mean mortal?" Mom didn't know, she never knew what dad was. Things just keep getting more confusing. "We don't age. Didn't you realize it? How old are you right now Ad?" "I'm older than I look mom, let's leave it at that." Watching her mother taking a step back, and the confusion on her face, like she was pondering something but didn't want to let the cat out of the bag. "It should have set in already. But what I don't understand is why you don't know this. Why haven't I told you?"

"Something's about the future are better left unknown even to your mom. I don't mean to be

cruel but I can't change the past, but my future is riding on it." Feeling herself begin to fade, "I

love you mom, never forget that."

Seeing her younger self emerging down the hallways, skipping happily, to their mother.

Why hadn't she remembered it growing up? Had she every questioned seeing the woman fade from the kitchen? She couldn't remember.

"I love you too Ad, you're stronger than you think, remember that..." Resting her hand on

Adrianna's young shoulder, staring down as she came up and hugged her leg. Nina wondered what the future held for her daughter. With a fade, there was someone that they had to pay a visit to.

Hitting the side of the walls out of frustration, Adrianna found herself back in her prison,

still no closer to finding out her truth. The glimpses were just teasing her, there was more to it.

There were even more questions now, like how did she just jump through time? There were so many things. What in the world were those stories that her mother used to tell her? How did they go? Knowing that she wasn't going to get the answers that she needed tonight, Adrianna decided to close her eyes and get some sleep. Since her mother used to tell her the stories before bed, maybe some sleep was just what she needed to remember. Whether she wanted to or not, Adrianna's body needed to rest, and she knew it. She would be no good to anyone if should couldn't function properly.

Her mother said that she was stronger than she knew; man, she didn't have any idea.

First, her mother kept the fact that she could jump time and was immortal from her father.

And her father didn't tell her mother that he was a witch and immortal as well. So, if neither of them knew about each other, she was going to go nowhere fast learning about what she could do.

Resting her head on her arm, trying to remember the stories of her childhood, she drifted off into a sound sleep. Letting exhaustion take her over. People always say that your dream can bring you clarity, here's hoping Adrianna thought.

She could hear her mother talking to her, telling her the story of the princess who could control her destiny. She would be able to change the outcome of her situations. If she told a fib, she would jump back a second in time and give the right answer. She had watched her older brother gets into trouble all the time for keeping the truth from her parents and didn't want that. She had wanted to be truthful and honest. Every time that she would jump in time, she would run and tell her parents so they wouldn't get mad. Jumping was not forbidden but you should have a good reason to do so. The princess liked to jump, she liked to visit friends of old and find things she had lost along the way. She didn't like the fact that she would never age.

Some of her mortal friends knew her secret, even though it was against her code. But,
she didn't want them scared when she just popped up. As her friends began to become elderly,
she almost wished that she was with them. They had found their loved ones, had a family,
grandchildren, and she was by herself. She just wanted her own happiness. Living forever didn't mean a world of happiness, not for everyone. And she felt that there wasn't any for her.

How could she be happy, if she could watch the people, she has grown to care about pass on? She couldn't save them from this fate, but she could bring them peace. Knowing that she would check in on the families over the years. Even if their children didn't know her, her friends felt that she was like an angel looking out for them and could rest easy. And the princess could grant that wish for her friends because it was truly one of the only things she could do.

After many years had gone by, and her friends were no more, she had met a man. A
handsome, intelligent young man. He looked to be around the same age as she looked, and for that she envied him. She had wished that she didn't age so that they could be together. The princess knew that it wasn't to happen, she decided to live in the moment. She just never counted on falling in love with him. As the years went on, she had to leave. The princess couldn't live with the fact of him not being with

her. So, she began to jump back in time. Knowing the outcome, she didn't have a fear of him discovering her secret.

The more times that she ventured back to see him, the more that she loved him. After the last time, the princess didn't know what happened, she just left and was never to return, not remembering who the man was. Wiped from her memory his name and image, but the feeling of love remained. Only remembering he was mortal, but unsure of even the year she conceived. Jumping forward to be safe. With her forever she would carry a piece of him; she would protect it with her soul. Her special child would grow up until she was frozen into her immortality.

One day when she could, her child would learn the truth. Always having a piece of his heart, close by would do. She might not have been able to be with him forever, his image forever hazy in her mind's eye, his name lost through time unable to remember why, but at least she had her joy. A child to share all her secret and powers with, to hold them close to their heart.

Startling herself, Adrianna woke up. The story, it was her mother's. She never knew that they could be together. All of this could have been different. All of this can be different.
Adrianna just had to get out. 'I will get out.'
"Oh, no you won't." said the voice from across the room.

Serina was back, this should be fun, or not. Adrianna had to tread carefully if everything was going to work in her favor. At least she didn't know what the dream was about, which Ad was grateful for. She only knew that 'Holly' wanted to escape. Still not knowing what or who she was, Ad needed to relax. Her day was just getting started.

"If you think that you could escape me, you're more of a fool than I first thought. No one ever leaves unless I decide it. As for you, you don't have hope. Luc will be mine and there is

nothing that you can do about it."

"If you couldn't get Luc to care about you before, what in the hell makes you think that he will

care about you now?" Knowing that she was walking a very thin line, Adrianna wanted to push just a little to see exactly what Serina knew.

"You miserable little tramp. Do you honestly think that Luc could love someone as simple-minded and young as you? You are a mortal; you don't know the first thing about him or his world. You will never be free, and he will never find you. My prisons are inescapable. Just ask the old woman, she has been here for over three hundred years. If she can't escape,

what makes you think that you can? I'll just watch you grow old and wither away to dust."

"What are you talking about; you don't know the first thing about love or compassion. If you did, you would have realized that trapping the people that he loves, is the quickest way of losing him. Luc values his family above everything else. And he will find us, all of us. And if you don't think so, then you are delusional." Just a little further, she just needed Serina rattled.

Gazing around her room full of all her acquisitions, Serina had no qualms about what she had done. Luc was never going to find out the lengths that she would go. If she had to keep him trapped for centuries for him to realize that she was the one for him, she would. Nothing was going to stop her, nothing she thought.

Maybe that's what Serina had to do. She had the tramp now, maybe she could use her as bait. If she meant that much to Luc, maybe he would come after her. She could capture him and then set Holly free. It wasn't like she would ever find her way back here. That would be impossible.

Now all she needed was a plan, some way to drop her guard enough for Luc to get through, but no one else. If her father found out that his precious nephew was missing, and she was the cause.... she didn't even go there; she was already on her dads pissed off list.

She had taken care of her brother all those years ago. Everyone just assumed that he had taken off. In a manner of speaking, he did, she just gave him a little help on his way. Where she sent him, they weren't going to find him. He would want the most revenge if he freed himself from his prison. He wasn't strong enough for that. Serina had bound his powers so tightly it's a wonder that he had survived this long. Looking around and smirking, she knew that Sebastian could see her, but she couldn't let the others know where he was. His place was special. She had stumbled across its years ago, uninhabited except for him.

A spell her mother had used for an emergency, just left sitting there. It was an emergency when she had used it. Her darling brother was about to ruin all her hard work. She couldn't think of a better place to trap him. It had to be one of the most perfect places she could have thought of. Flipping her hair over her shoulder, because that had always bothered him, her whatever attitude. She was enjoying the moment, imagining everything he must be saying on the other side.

AWAKEN THE FLAMES

CHAPTER FOURTEEN

"What do you mean my mother has been missing for centuries? How could that happen, no one was that daring." Sal was in disbelief; someone has been able to take his mother. He wasn't sure if that bothered him more, or the fact that no one had told him.

"Yes, sir. She went out on an errand that day and never returned. We didn't want to cause alarm by telling everyone. Then our enemies would think us weak with her missing. She is the most powerful of us all, the only way for something to happen to her, was if she was injured."

"So, you are telling me that all this time, you have been lying to everyone, and no one has seen her." Looking at the people they had with them, they all had an idea who would do such a thing.

"Did she have any visitors before she disappeared?"

"Only her granddaughter, she came and spent a few weeks prior to her going. But Serina left a few days before. We never heard from either of them again."

"Did Serina leave anything behind when she was here? What room did she stay in?" Mary knew that Serina was up to no good. But hurting her own grandmother, the most powerful of all the witches. She could control the cardinal signs, all of them. What had Serina done to her for her to become weak enough to get caught?

"She stayed in the room adjoining her grandmothers. She said she wanted to spend as much

time with her as she could."

"Adjoining room? That's how. She must have done something while she slept." Sal muttered

to himself.

Not only had Serina taken Adrianna, but now her grandmother was also missing. Luc had more reason than ever to panic. If Serina was powerful enough to trap her grandmother; then they were on a whole other playing field. Leaving his mother's, Sal and everyone went back to the office, to figure out the best way to handle the situation. Everyone knew that this had just gone from bad, to unimaginable.

Serina was causing more trouble than they knew what to do with. Her undoing was coming soon and Luc was going to make sure that he was the one to do it. Where would Serina have taken them, and what else has she done over the years?

Sal was pissed, Mary was fuming, and the guys were itching for a fight. With Serina having this much plotting over the years, they really didn't know what they were going to be getting into. They had to be prepared for anything. Everyone's safety depended on this. One step at a time, that's all any of them could do. They just hoped that Adrianna and her grandmother would be safe enough until they would be able to get to them.

\#   \#   \#

"I have special plans for you Holly, just wait. You will see your Luc
again soon, but not for long. But enjoy your stay while you can,
because once Luc gets here, you're on your way out."
"If that's what you think. Luc won't leave here without me and I won't
leave here without him.
You picked the wrong people to deal with this time."
"When I get back things are going to change. Make certain of that.
Don't take my threats lightly, you have no idea."

With that, Serina left again. Adrianna looked around quickly and
had seen enough. She knew that she needed help. She had to ask
Christina there wasn't a choice.
"I need your help; I need to learn how to control my powers. I can free
us all from this, but I
have no control over my powers. Please, will you help me?"
"She will end you before you even know what happened. Holly, you
can't. The only people she can't trap is her family. There is no
escaping."
"I am her family; she just doesn't know it."
"What are you talking about; there was only her and Sebastian. And
she put him on another prison years ago. He is the only one who could
free us."
"No. I am her half-sister; she just never knew about me. My mother
left Sal the day she found out she was pregnant, but she didn't know at

the time. Sal never told Serina or Sebastian about me. He didn't trust Serina not to try and hurt me or my mother. He kept it to himself while he looked for us. It's a very long story, but please, I need your help to free us all. I know what I

can do. I just can't control it."

"If you are who you say you are, then there might be some hope. What can you do? I know

about the fire, but there is something else, I just can't figure it out." Christina knew that Holly had something special about her, she just needed to know what.

"I can control fire. I can bring it forward and feel it rush through my body. I have always known when something is going to happen before it does. And I can jump through time. Not for long.

Just a few moments here and there; I just need to concentrate on where I want to go."

"Witches can't jump through time. What else are you?"

"My mother was a time shifter; she was able to go back and forth between time and realms. She figured out a way to stay in places longer. But she died before she taught me how to use it. I

just discovered it the other night. I suddenly saw her in front of me from a scene when I was a

child. I didn't tell her that she vanished, not wanting to chance fate."

"So, all we have to do is teach you to call your elements when you need them and how to use them. Charles, we need the old woman to help us. She needs to know."

"Christina, why is she so important. How can she help."

"Holly...."

"My name is Adrianna, but please, don't tell Serina. The less she knows, the better for all of

us."

"Adrianna, I agree. Serina doesn't need any more power that she already has. As for the old woman, she has the power to control all five elements, she could teach you to control fire better than either of us, she is your grandmother. I am sure you are the one that the elders talk about.

But there are four of you that are special. The fire is the strongest. And you would all descend from her bloodline. But your elements would only come forth in a great time of need. And I think that the time has come."

"My grandmother? She's here? But I thought Serina couldn't trap her family?"

"Serina weakened her, she's hurt and not regenerating that's the only reasons she is trapped."

There was just so much going on in such a short time. Adrianna's mind was racing with all the different information. One thing was sure; she and Christina were going to make sure that Serina didn't hurt anyone else.

If her grandmother was truly here, then she would have to tread carefully around her sister. Whatever sister dearest was up to, it was about to come to an end. But, why take her grandmother? Adrianna couldn't understand that. What did her grandmother have to do with Luc? Why was her sister picking off members of her own family? There were so many different reasons that Serina could be doing any of this. It had to be something else, something that she just wasn't getting.

Adrianna wasn't going to rest until she found out though. It wouldn't matter how long it will take; she would find out all her siblings secrets. Freeing all those who had recently joined her family, and there was going to be nothing that Serina could do about any of it.

It had seemed like days had passed, instead of hours. The time was dragging. But Ad was sure, that it was the magic, the spell was working. It kept her confused, over thinking her moves. She needed to get to the old women, knew that she could help her. If the woman was truly her grandmother, she just might have the answers that Adrianna needed. Being trapped in the frame wasn't helping her. She couldn't time shift to see her because as far as Ad had known, she never met the woman before, and didn't have a place in time to focus on.

There had to be another way, she needed her mother to help her. She had already gone back in time a couple of times in the past few hours. Not knowing if she was doing any damage, Ad was unsure if she should risk a jump so soon. Her mother may begin to catch on and start asking questions. Having so many new questions of her own, she wished that she could tell her mother the truth about her father. If they hadn't discovered about each other up until this point, she was sure that there was a very good reason behind it.

Adrianna believed in fate and destiny or whatever it was called. Why it stuck her in this situation, she would never know. She was a strong believer in "you only get what you can handle." Someone was having a good laugh she thought. If someone out there thinks she can do this, then she would prove them right. All she knew was that Serina was a complete psycho.

Someone who trapped their own grandmother put their brother in another prison, and captured the parents of the man that she supposedly loved; needed some serious professional help. And not the cheap kind either Did they have help for witches? Using the term loosely, it would have to be somewhere they couldn't use their powers. Imagining a room full of pissed off witches. Just the thought sent chills along her spine.

"Christina, how do we get the old woman, I mean my grandmother's attention? She probably doesn't even know about me. What do I do, say 'HI I KNOW THAT WE NEVER MET, BUT I AM YOU GRANDDAUGHTER AND NEED A LITTLE HELP.' We need to come up with something, and she is so far away."

"Charles is working on it; he has been up all day trying to come up with something. As soon as he does, I will let you know. Have you been practicing calling your power?"

"Not yet, just can't believe fate would think that this would be a good test for me. They

couldn't come up with anything better?" Adrianna could handle an all-
out shopping spree, or a room full of animals, but this?

"You know the saying, she works in mysterious ways. There is a good
reason for this. I

am sure but she'll only reveal herself when the time is right. And for
that, you must be

patient Adrianna."

"Do you think it would be safe if I jumped back to see my mother.
Maybe pry for a few

answers about the time shifting?"

"As long as you don't ask too many questions or give too many
answers about the future.

Just choose the place you go wisely so that you get the most out of it.
And be safe."

"I will and thanks Christina for everything. When we get out of her, I
will help you

look for Matteo no matter how long it takes us to find him."

Taking time to consider where she should shift to, Adrianna
knew that she had to make it right. There were so many special times
when she was growing up. Mom had always made sure that
everything was a memory. Maybe that was it? Maybe this was part of
mom's past? Maybe when she jumped, she already knew that this was
going to happen, that's why certain memories stand out more than
others? Her mom was leaving a path for her to follow. But what time

to go back to? There were so many occasions. Which one, which one to choose?

She felt like she was banging her head against a wall. There were so many times in her childhood. How do you choose just one point? She needed to determine which time had the answers. Why couldn't just one time stand out above all others? Something special, something that was different from everything else?
"That's it!"

As if overhead an imaginary light bulb just clicked on. She knew where to go; she knew what place. Why didn't she see it earlier? There was a path. The stories all ended the same way. There was a specific conversation, and then there was a different story one night. As if they were in order.

Her mother had left a detailed course for her to follow. Now all she had to do was get to the right place at the right time. What if she was wrong, just wanting to see something that wasn't there? She had to follow her instincts, they wouldn't lead her astray.

What did she have to lose? She could put the pieces together without her mother being any wiser. But if mom was as old as she thought; there had to be more to it.

She was missing something. What was it? What was that missing piece of the puzzle?
Remembering the part of the story about the princess' family, how they wanted her to be different. It wasn't her mother that they wanted to be different. It was Adrianna.

The trip they took. Her mother made her take some medication before they left; mom said it was to relax her. When she woke up, she didn't remember how she got there. Then the same thing happened when they got home. Her mother jumped with her when she was a child. Back to her own world. Things seemed strange when she was a child. Like she was somewhere she wasn't supposed to be, it had left her feeling unease, even the memory now brought forward the same feelings.

That woman they stayed with, what was her name? The woman was so nice and sweet. She said that she was the most special little princess in the entire world. One day soon, she would find out how special she truly was. She said that Ad could do anything she wanted; she was blessed with many gifts. Did she know? Who was she? She had to go back to that day to find out. She just hoped that whatever she was doing to jump was the right thing because if not, who knew where she would end up.

Concentrating on the lush green grasses of the gardens, the warm breeze blowing through the trees, Adrianna could feel herself moving through time. This time she was watching it as if you were watching a movie in freeze frame. She could see all the parts of her life; she could make out each moment. Every memory she had ever had, and there was the one that she wanted. The memories before her laid out like a book. Feeling as if all she had to do was reach and grab it. Before she could even blink, she was in the garden.

Adrianna could hear the soft currents of the brook running in the distance. She could feel the warm breeze as it ruffled the leaves on the trees. Smelling the flowers as she walked past; the roses and daisies. There were rows and rows of daisies as if they were planted for her. Reaching down to touch one she could feel the velvety softness of the petals, the firm stem and the crispness of the leaves. This was her home; she knew it with every piece of her.

As she strolled further down the path, there were stone benches and statues, each of them searching for things to come, guarding the treasures within. Her feet found the cobblestone path that she remembered as a child and the stone wall that trimmed it. It had seemed so much higher when she was younger, but now it barely came to the middle of her thighs. How things seemed so much different when she was a child. ust as beautiful though like a place untouched by time.

On one of the benches sat a familiar woman, one she recognized from her past. Not knowing what to do exactly. This woman might not recognize her for who she is. Trying to determine how to approach her, Ad wasn't prepared for her to know who she was. By the look on the woman's face, she knew exactly who Ad was and she was happy to see her.

"It's not nice to just stand there and stare Adrianna, why don't you come and sit down?"

"Um, pardon me. Did you just call me Adrianna, my name is...."

"I know who you are darling. So, you don't have to worry about startling me. I have been waiting for you for a very long time."

Feeling a little unsure of the new situation she was in, to say that Ad didn't expect that reaction would be an understatement. She followed the woman's request, knowing that no harm could come to her because her time was limited.

"Hello, I am sorry that I don't remember your name. You know who and what I am then? Do you also know why I am here?"

"Yes, my dear. Nothing ever gets past me. To say that you found yourself in a little bit of a mess, would be a vast understatement. You knew to come here in great times of need So, tell me what has happened?"

"But won't that change to course of the future?"

"My dear, we are in a different realm, what has already been done I am aware of. But unfortunately, I can only guide you, not give you the answers that you seek."

"So why did I know to come here if you can't help me?"

"When you were brought here as a child, it was so that you knew that it would be a safe place for you. Your mother wanted you to know that you could always come here if you needed to. There were times when you would just show up when you were younger. But we would have to do a quick fix to make you forget. Now is your time to be here. Nothing can harm you here, you are safe."

The woman just smiled with all the warmth of the sun. She was more beautiful than anyone Adrianna had ever seen, and she knew that she spoke the truth. She couldn't be much older than Adrianna herself, but now knowing about immortals she couldn't be entirely sure. With everything she had learned of the last few weeks, Ad knew never to judge things as they seem.

"How many times have I been here? I don't remember. And please tell me who are you? I remember you, but not who you are?" There were so many answers that she needed,

but didn't know how much time she would have to get them.

"I am your aunt Lucia. You were named after me Adrianna Lucia. You are very special. Where you are? It the place where your mother grew up. Your mother thought it would be a safe place for you. She found me when I was a very young immortal and had a knack for getting into trouble. She saved me and brought me here, but she never knew that I was your aunt. My brother is your father, but I never told her that. I will not mess with Fate and her determination. She is fickle, to begin with, and would not like to be on her bad side.

That's how I ended up here. I used to think that it would be fun to play with the air and the currents. The breezes were my favorite. Your mother knew that I was a witch and knew that there were horrible people trying to capture me. She brought me here to keep me safe. Even though I wasn't with my family, I knew that it was for the best, and have lived here ever since. Your mother though was completely unaware of who your father truly was. I didn't want to be the one to tell her. When she brought you here as a child and you spent a few days, I knew that there was more to you than I first thought. Tell me, Adrianna, what is your special gift?"

"My gift. Fire, I can call fire."

"And that's where your family came from the elements and shifting. Strange I know. That way you knew to find your way back, but I didn't tell her about your gift. You can control fire, or you are just learning too. I bound your powers when you were here because you had a habit of setting the shrubs on fire. I knew that your mother didn't know the full truth of your lineage, so I needed to keep you safe."

"How is it that I am here for so long, usually by this point, I am returning to my time."

"When you jump back in time, it is true; you are only allowed a few moments to fix things. But when you jump realms, the same rules don't apply. You don't know much and therefore can't change anything. And when you return to your time, it will move the same as it was before."

"So, I have no time limit here? If Serina realizes that I am gone it wouldn't be good."

There would be a whole lot of trouble when she went back, and Adrianna knew
that for sure.

"When you jump, a piece or a shadow of you stays behind, did you not know that? Your
mother should have told you, she told me all the rules just in case......Adrianna, where's

your mother?" Lucia was beginning to dread the answer. It had been so long since Nina had come back to visit, and her brother had seemed rather smug the last few years, she was getting a sick feeling in the pit of her stomach, which was never good.

With the question Adrianna broke down, she finally had someone who knew what she was the entire time to talk to. Sitting down and telling her aunt Lucia the entire story. Of how her mother died, meeting Luc, and what her so-called sister had done.

Even though she had Luc to talk with, having now met her aunt gave her a piece of a family that was missing for so long; feeling a sense of comfort. Memories of meeting Lucia came rushing back to Adrianna, remembering when she was a child, and the smile her aunt would give her. Hearing everything and realizing that Adrianna and all of them were in more trouble than they knew. Lucia had her work cut out for her. Her niece was going to disrupt the entire balance of things and didn't even know it. She and Adrianna had to get started.

Ad needed to be able to use her full powers, and with Lucia's help, that shouldn't take too long. Lucia could help her free her grandmother, Christina, and Charles. She'd teach that spoiled brat of a niece of hers a good lesson. Fate had put Lucia and Adrianna in their positions for a reason and that reason just came clear. They had to stop Serina, before the whole reality as all immortals knew it, would come to a halt.

Adrianna's fire and passion; would make sure that it would all work out. Her niece would be the one to set things right. Lucia just needed to help her train. Things that usually took years, she would only have mere weeks or even days to figure out.

Lucia wished she had her mother's guidance. Even though she hadn't seen her mother since she was younger, her mother would know that she was safe. A mother would do anything to protect her children. Her older brother didn't visit much, and only met her half-brother once: she was the only sibling to know about him, having been sent away after he was born to keep him safe.

Whoever was causing trouble didn't just start over the last few hundred years. Whether Serina was in with them or not, they would have to been figured out. Once Adrianna could free her, her grandmother and anyone else caught up in this mess, Lucia would get to the bottom of this. She had all her powers and knew how to control them. With her niece's help, they would get this finished.

CHAPTER FIFTEEN

She was concentrating on something, which meant the bond that he had with her was only getting stronger. He knew that she was thinking about him, knew that she was trying to draw energy from his memory. Promising himself to her was one of the best things he had done, even if she would hate him for it. It was going to be their only chance of getting Ad and her grandmother to safety.

With each passing moment, his feelings for her grew deeper. He wanted her with him, beside him, in his life; wanted a future, wanted to spoil her. Wanting to make up for all the years that she went without. Even though she would fight him in saying that she didn't. Deep down, he could feel her sorrow for the years she had lost; and he was going to spend eternity making it up to her.

Each year that they enter together, would be the beginning of another lifetime. He would make sure each one was filled with love and happiness. Maybe one day they would have a family of their own. Love and knowledge passed down to their family. But first, he had to get her back, and then explain why he did what he did.

"Mary she's planning something." Luc could feel her emotions. Knew that something was up

sensing the inner turmoil that was before her.

"Do you think she will try to escape? Does she even realize that if the two of you concentrate enough, we could find her easier?"

"I don't think that she knows yet that I can help her. As soon as she realizes it, things will go a lot faster." Praying that Adrianna would figure it out soon.

"I am going to go to my place for a few. Maybe I can get through to her, maybe, but I need quiet

to do it with no distractions."

"Text if you need anything, and Luc, be careful. You're our only tie to her right now. We need you in the best possible shape to help her."

"I know Mary. We will get her back. I won't rest until we do."

"Wear this while you're gone. Just in case. Think of it as a homing beacon."

Taking a necklace from her pocket, placing it close to her heart. Focusing her energy into it, as she compressed it with her hand. The ruby necklace was powerful; she knew it belonged with Luc for the moment. Placing it around his neck giving him a nod, she let him know that he was safe to go.

"Thank you, I won't take it off."

Vanishing from the office and reappearing back in his apartment he needed to think. Running his hands through his hair and making his way towards the fireplace with the continuous firing burning within. Resting his hands on the mantel his head hung low. Rolling his necking trying to ease the tension from his body, he opened his eyes glancing into the mirror and realizing he wasn't alone. Feeling his blood beginning to boil beneath the surface. How dare she show up here.

"Serina, funny seeing you here." With malice laced in his voice, he spat out the words like fire at her.

She sat there, on his leather wing-backed chair, wearing a pair of fitted jeans and a low-cut shirt, her outfit screamed easy-lay all over it. He could feel his body tighten with aggression, just looking at of her. He needed to keep his cool if he gave anything away; it could mean Adrianna's life.

He watched as she eased herself up from the chair and ran her finger along the top of the mantel walking towards him. Anyone else it would seem sexy, on her it looked desperate. Crossing the distance between them, she placed a hand on his shoulder, pressing her body into his. Just the closeness was making him ill. He could feel her breath on his neck, as it sent chills down his spine. She wanted something from him, but what she was demanding, he wouldn't give up.

"Hello Luc, I have your girlfriend. If you would like to see her, I suggest that you come with me. No tricks, I really don't have the patience for it. Your girlfriend is trying enough." She breathlessly whispered in his ear.

"Serina, you're still the most miserable, stubborn conniving bitch. You have no soul."

"Funny, your girlfriend said the same thing."

Bringing him closer to her, she ran her hands down his arms digging her nails in as if to get a better hold. Spinning him around, their lips were mere inches apart, Serina grabbed a hold of him and both were gone. He was just thankful that he was wearing his cousin's ruby; Mary didn't do things for no reason.

Finding himself in Serina's place didn't sit well. This was the one place he never wanted to be. Yet at the same time, it was the place he had to be to find Adrianna. He hoped that Adrianna was safe, and no harm had come to her. He would never harm a woman, but Serina fell out of that category a long time ago. Luc knew that he shouldn't say too much, unsure of what Serina already knew. He would let her lead the conversation, treading carefully.

Taking stock of his surrounding, wanting to be completely aware of every possibility. Too many things could happen. The smallest thing could set the unspeakable into motion. The room was small but cozy looking. Overlooking the fireplace there was a small couch, with a blanket across it. A chaise lounge, and if you sat on it just right, you had a wonderful view of the city; too bad it was wasted on her.

Some flowers on the mantel, with an abstract print above it. The room was the color of moss, sinister but inviting, it was meant to draw you in, but you wouldn't return. Books of witchcraft and spells on top of the coffee table. If you didn't know better, you would think that you walked into the house of a collector. Knowing better, he was in a house of horrors. He could feel the pain radiating around him. A normal person wouldn't pick up on any of it, but he sensed the pain in everything. Nothing in these rooms was hers, to begin with. It was all stolen.

There was more here than he was seeing. Serina, she just stood there staring at him. Not saying anything. Just watching as he looked around, knowing full well what he was doing.

"You can't get out, so don't even try. There is no escape."

"What do you want Serina, I know that you have Sal's mom and...."

"Holly, I have your Holly. Is that what you were going to say?"

"Yes, Holly." At least she didn't know her real name for that he was thankful.

"I want you Luc, and I have told you that continually. All this could have been avoided. I just
wanted you."

Watching her, as if a spoiled child throwing a tantrum. Always wanted her own way with no regard for others. Standing twirling her hair, pulling the silky strands through the pads of her fingers, trying to soothe herself, something she had done as long as he'd known her.

"You don't want me. You want to control me. Sorry, I don't think so. Now where is Holly, Serina? What have you done with her?" Trying to gain space, he pushed her back knocking her off her feet making her stumble. He could sense that he'd just pissed her off, but she was getting a little too close for his liking.

"She's in a safe place. Don't worry; she can't bother anyone where she is. And you won't be seeing her. She has been quite useful. If I didn't see the two of you together, I might
never have been able to reach you."

"Reach me; you're just as crazy as ever! Now, where is HOLLY?"

Holly, Holly, Holly! What did that bitch have that she didn't? Oh, he wasn't going to see her any more that was for sure she thought to herself. Luc wasn't going to ever see her again. Maybe she would keep them both for a while. As long as it takes, until he finally realizes that Serina is the one for him.

Feeling the energy well up inside of her, she extended her arms and let Luc feel the power she had. It had developed well over the centuries. Just a little force nothing too much, but it was enough to send him hurtling back into the mirror. She stood there gloating over him. If he wanted to learn the hard way, it would make it all the more fun for her.

"Luc, I told you, you're not going to see her again." With that, she threw another volley of energy, his way. There was enough force that it left him limp on the floor.

"I will…" was all he managed to get out before a cloud of darkness overtook him. He knew that she was putting a spell on him, but he couldn't react.

Kneeling beside him, she brushed the hair off his forehead. Gazing at him knowing that she had won for the moment.

"Don't worry Luc; I will take good care of you." Smirking as she left the room, he wasn't going anywhere for a few hours at least. Leaving him sprawled out on the floor, until she returned with what she needed.

She waited patiently as the time passed. Dreaming of the life they would share together. The pair would be unstoppable. Having waited for centuries to have him, Serina was willing to wait for a few more till he came around. He would see things her way, even if she had to beat it into him. Luc would be hers. The pesky mortal would only live for so long. He'll morn her and then eventually move on. They all do with time. Watching as he begun to stir, her thoughts moved back to the present and what she needed to do.

"Where in the hell?"

Looking around the room to see his surroundings, Luc couldn't believe it. He knew that Serina was crazy, but this was a little too much. When he first arrived at her apartment, it looked somewhat normal for a witch's place, that is. But now as he looked, he was so wrong.

The four poster beds edges rose to the ceiling. The dark wood only adding to the eeriness of the room. Chains across his arms and legs, holding him firmly in place. Struggling to gain freedom, their restraints only tightening more with each thrash. It was impossible. The shelves were lined with bottles of elixirs and roots, books lined another wall, and some were in languages that he couldn't even understand. What was she up to? There had to be more to it than he first thought. Someone doesn't go through this much trouble unless they have an ulterior motive. Just what hers was, Luc had to find out.

Where was Adrianna, he couldn't feel her emotions anywhere? What had Serina done? He couldn't let on that he knew that she wasn't around. Maybe Serina didn't know? She didn't know that they were connected, the longer that he kept it that way, the better. He had to keep Adrianna safe no matter what.

There had to be something here that he could use. Something? There was just so much crap lying around, he didn't know where to look first. He just hoped Mary and the guys will hold off looking for him long enough for Adrianna to return, from wherever she was. Not that he really wanted her anywhere near Serina, but he needed to be sure that she was safe.

"I see you have woken up darling, and how was your sleep? You dreamed of me I hope."

"Don't ever call me darling again, you crazy miserable bitch."

"You'll learn to feel the same about me as I feel about you Luc, we belong together. We have always belonged together. You'll see, we are meant to be." Forcefully pushing herself up from the couch, hesitating for only a moment. Serina couldn't let her anger get the better of her,

not now. Not when she was so close.

"The only place that you are meant to be is in the psycho ward Serina. They have special rooms for people like you and they have pretty white padded walls." Luc knew that he shouldn't be egging her on, but she was crazy, and he needed to get free to help Adrianna.

Laughing at Luc, Serina knew that once Holly was taken care of, there was nothing standing in her way. She had all the time in the world. Making her way towards the bed, seductively peeling off her clothes as she walked. Luc could feel the bile rising in his throat. If she thought that they would ever be together like that, she was insane. He had to stay calm though, couldn't get any angrier than he already was.

It would put Ad in jeopardy. The thought of Serina, lying beside him, no matter how attractive Serina was, she was nothing compared to Adrianna.

Serina was sinister, Adrianna was all warmth. Serina would use her body as a

weapon and wouldn't think twice about it. Adrianna was too shy and delicate too; she was built for love. Hope and happiness radiated off Adrianna after she discovered the truth. He didn't think Serina even knew what real love ever was. She only wanted things to be a prize. Once she got what she wanted, she would be on to her next conquest.

As she rounded the bed to be beside him, it was like she was in a dream. This was what she had waited her whole life for. Standing there, and yet he wouldn't even look at her. All the work she had gone through, all the effort. He wouldn't even show her the respect that she deserved. She would make him want her, make him ache for her. She would have to remove that protection spell off him first. She just had to find a way. Then she would enthrall him to love her. Sometimes love just needs a boost. Looking at him, it would only be a matter of time. She always got what she wanted.

"You can fight it, for now, Luc, but hear me when I say, one day you will be mine." Leaving him lying on the bed, he couldn't go anywhere so she didn't have to worry.

#   #   #

Feeling from the charm that something happened to her cousin, Mary knew that they had to act fast. First, she had to fill the guys in on what was going on and then she had to look for Luc. The ruby she gave him had a tracking spell on it.

"Mary, we have to get him."

"Paul, shut up I know. But she has him somewhere and I can't pinpoint it."

"Would you just find him already!"

"Now who is the edgy one, Vince?"

"Both of you shut up." Mary needed to concentrate. She gave Luc the ruby for something. He needed it and needed to be protected. For how long it would hold up against Serina, Mary didn't know.

The ruby's energy was transferred into parts. One-part energy, and the other strength. He needed both right now. She could locate the energy. Mary wanted to give him time. He could find Ad and the grandmother and help them get out. With Paul and Vince sitting on the couch discussing different possibilities, they needed to be prepared for anything. If only Sebastian was here, this was his strong point.

He could plan anything. Wherever he was, she was sure that only Serina knew. Her sister Elena had been missing him for too long and Mary would do anything to help her find him. But that could wait for now. First, she needed to find Luc and Adrianna.

"Mary, have you found him yet?"

"Nothing, wherever she took him, he is heavily protected. It shouldn't be much longer. The crystal is strong, only another few minutes and we should have something, Vince."

"Vince, Mary, do you feel it?"

"What Paul, what's going on?"

Letting himself absorb the influences of nature, Paul knew that things were happening. He couldn't explain it but something or someone was not where they should be. But who? He needed more information. He just wished that he could figure it out first so that everyone could be in position.

The faster that they did this, the better they would all be. When he got his hand on Serina, she would pay. He kept his identity from his friends for their safety, if they ever found out the truth. He spent his whole life making sure no one knew his dirty little secret. This witch wasn't going to be the one to oust him. A few hours, they still had a few hours until Paul's panic would set in.

"Got him! Hang on Luc; we are coming to get you."

"Where is he, Mary, do we have enough time?"

"Paul, is everything in order, is everyone ready?"

"Vince and I know what to do. As for Uncle Sal, he will meet us when we get back. One shock for Serina is enough at first, there are other people to watch out for until we have her. And if she gets away, the last person she needs to know is helping us is her father."

"Agreed, are the two of you ready?" Mary was worried for not only Luc but Adrianna as well. If Serina didn't know about their connection yet, they were going to keep it from her if they could. Serina was just a hell of a lot closer than either of the guys realized, this one was going to be a shocker.

"Ok, Mary, what's the address? Let's get Luc back and then find Adrianna."

"Let's just say that we don't have that far to go."

Both Paul and Vince were looking at Mary like she had grown a second head. How close could they possibly be? Maybe they should go after Luc and Adrianna both at the same time.

"Um, Mary. Where exactly are, are we going?" Paul needed details.

"How close are we talking Mary?"

"How's two floors down." They both just looked at her now. How could they have been so close and never realized it? Two floors below this whole time, all these years with not even noticing. Serina was using some powerful magic. This had bad written all over it.

"So, what are we waiting for, let's go get our boy back."

Seeing his friends flash in on the other side of the room, Luc wondered how they found him, knowing Mary, she had her ways. Now all he had to do to keep his friends safe was focus Serina's attention on him. If she had, she was doing a great job of hiding it.

"Luc, why do you fight it? You know that we are meant to be together. It is destined; the daughter of the most powerful warlock would become the next powerful leader of the coven and would bring all the other covens together. Together, Luc, you and I will rule everyone. No one would dare cross our paths. Just think of it, all the power would be ours."

"She's nuts," Vince mouthed to Paul and Mary. The three of them knew that they had to stop her. They also knew that she wasn't the daughter that they were talking about. Adrianna would be the one to join all the covens, and Serina had just made that possible.

Looking at her accomplices they knew that the time to act was now.

"Hey Serina, I thought that I warned you before to stay away from the people that I cared about. Obviously, you don't listen to messages." Mary watched as she turned around in shock of someone being in the room.

"You again......why don't you mind your own business; this doesn't concern you so get lost." With that, she sent a powerful jolt of electricity at Mary, but Vince jumped out in front.

"Vince, no!" As he lay there lifeless on the floor, Mary was going to go at Serina with everything she had. No one or nothing was going to stop her.

"You just can't stay out of other people's business, can you? Who the hell are you anyway?"

"Your cousin, you self-righteous witch. And who made it OK for you to play ruler of the land?"

"The elders made me. What do you mean cousins? I know all my family and you are not in it." Serina said snakingly.

"That's exactly what I said when I found out that I was related to you. You give witches of all families, a really bad name." Looking down hopefully giving Vince enough time to recover, Mary never saw when Serina flashed her. Before she knew it, Mary was no longer in the apartment. More like looking at it through the window. Everyone was there but they couldn't see her.

"OOOHHH, this isn't good," Mary said to herself, realizing she was now in a whole lot of trouble, looking around, seeing Sebastian standing in front of her.

Not knowing where Mary had gone, Paul had mere seconds to free Luc, he just hoped that it was enough time. Vince was still down but he quickly bound Vince to himself so that his buddy wouldn't get left behind, then for Luc.

While Serina was gloating, and going over to check on Vince, she never realized that there was a third person with them. This was the window that he needed.

Quietly taking off the chain that held Luc, he grabbed a hold of his friend look over at
Vince just as Serina was getting close to him, and then all she heard was "Hey bitch, we are so out of here!" With that, he flashed out with his two friends back to Mary's apartment. If Serina hadn't found out that she was living next door to a witch for all these years, it was the safest place to be.

Paul and Luc were growing more concerned, Vince had been out for a while. The longer he was ou,t the worse it was going to be. He would have to thank Vince for helping Mary, and then would have to figure out where Mary was. The nightmare just kept getting worse. They could hear their friend beginning to stir, which was a good sign. "Vince. Buddy, come on snap out of it. Luc, how are you holding up?" Torn between helping both friends, Paul needed to make sure they both stayed out of trouble.

"Fine, but she still has Adrianna and now Mary, Vince is half KO'd so now what." Luc could feel his frustration growing.

"Well, at least we got you out. You seem to be the prize in the Cracker Jack box as far as Serina is concerned. We aren't that far from Serina's place so if we know that she is gone, we can go back."

"Paul, what do you mean we aren't that far from Serina's; this is Mary's place..." With the look that his friend was giving him, Luc knew there was more going on than he realized.

"Yea, conveniently Mary and Serina actually live in the same building. They never knew about each other. So, unless you can think of a better place to be, I would say this is it."

"Would you two ladies stop your bitching over there, it feels like I have just got run over by a Mac Truck. What the hell happened, and where is Mary?" Vince felt completely disoriented, and needed some answers. By the way, his two friends were passing looks between them, he knew he really didn't want to hear the answer.

AWAKEN THE FLAMES

CHAPTER SIXTEEN

"Argh...why can't I get it, Aunt Lucia? Every time I try and reach for the fire, it's like it goes in the other direction."

"Adrianna, don't try to get it, that's the problem. Fire is part of you and you are part of it.

Once you realize and understand that, the control is yours. Pretend that it is like your arm, an extension of your body. You don't need to ask for it for control, you need to feel it."

"But I am...."

"No, you're not! You are trying too hard. You don't have to try, it's already with you. I am going to completely unbind your powers, but it may be a little too much at first, but I think that it is the only way."

Knowing that her niece was going to be overwhelmed, Lucia didn't have a choice. If they were going to beat Serina, Adrianna needed every bit of power, she had. Hesitantly, looking at her Aunt; Was she ready for everything at once? She could barely control the little power she had. Trying to fight back the panic as it would not do her any good. Lucia was the only person she had right now. The only one who could help her. With a nod, Adrianna knew it was time. Letting Lucia's voice guide her, was their only chance.

"Adrianna, just lie down and try to relax. Don't think of anything; just let yourself feel the warmth surrounding you. Let the warmth envelope your body. Feel it rushing through every fiber and bonding with every piece of your being. It's part of you and has always been. The red heat of the fire runs through your veins, the orange of the flame burns through your organs and the deep blue center, the purist of the heat beats through your heart. You are fire, and fire is you. Together you are one, nothing or no one can ever take that away from you. This is your strength; this is what will allow you to beat Serina. Not you're magic, not your time shifting but you. You have all the strength that you need coursing through your veins.You're special, and you know it. Now let yourself feel it. Feel it, Adrianna."

As she listened to her aunt, Adrianna could feel the heat burn through her body. Letting her head drift from side to side, feeling the tingling in her fingers and toes. The warmth that infused itself with her spine, the release of tension from her shoulders, the slow fire that flared through every muscle.

It was part of her. Even with her eyes closed, she could see the shards of color fusing with her, being displayed like fireworks right in front of her. The strength that coursed through her, she was refreshed and renewed. This was the way she was supposed to feel, this was what had been missing all those years; she now felt complete.

She could feel her eyes fluttering as her aunt finished talking to her. Taking a moment, allowing herself to become accustomed to the changes. Even though they weren't visible on the outside, she could feel it coursing through the inside. She finally realized why she had never felt whole, like part of her, was missing.

When Lucia bound her powers, she also bound part of
Adrianna's being she thought. For so long she had searched, as though
she was looking for something lost. In fact, she had never lost it, it was
just tied up deep down inside, wanting to be freed. She truly felt free,
felt whole. She knew what had to be done. Aware of all her
surroundings, so acutely. The temperature, textures, everything the
earth had to offer she could sense. She could see and harness the heat
radiating off the earth. She was whole at last. Luc filled her heart, and
the fire fueled her soul.

The new-found hope in her. They would get through this.
Adrianna, Lucia and anyone else that bitch of a sister hurt, wouldn't
suffer anymore. The fire was a force to be reckoned with, and so was
she.
"Just wait, Serina, you may have started this, but we're going to finish
it."

With her aunt's teachings, Adrianna tried again. Remembering
everything that Lucia had told her. She envisioned the flame. Willing
it to be, and there, in her hand, she could see the shards of light appear.
Holding fire in the palm off her hand. Feeling as it bounce of her palm,
and flow through her fingers. It was graceful and elegant, the purity of
it. Rolling her hand around watching as it moved with her, through
her, extending up her body, encasing her completely.

Just like her aunt had said, it was an extension of her. It felt
right, looked right. Playing with it like a child and a ball, between her
hands and having complete control over it. Molding it with her

thoughts, whatever she wanted it would transform into. A bird, leaf, dagger all the visions amplified. Closing it off and bringing it forth again.

Nothing had ever felt so amazing. Always wondering why, she had been obsessed with the Phoenix, now she knew why it was as if the Phoenix was part of her.

She let different emotions wash over her and watched the flame's reaction. The way it intensified when she was angry, the way it flourished when she was happy. It would be a weapon against her sister, but truly would be a gift. With Lucia controlling the wind and currents, and oxygen-fed fire, together...just the thought.

"Aunt Lucia, can I use this, and the people feel the heat, but not the burn?"

"Yes, whatever you envision, it will become. But it's up to you if they feel the pain or pleasure from it. You could summon a dagger and use it as such, but it would just be a dagger unless you willed it otherwise."

"So, I will be able to control how it's used then?" "Yes, whatever you want it, it will be."

Lucia knew that she had done the right thing, Adrianna had full control. She didn't even need the lesson; all she truly needed was the freedom. The histories were right. When they said, the elements would be yielded to those who knew how to use them with ease. If she was air, and Adrianna was fire, then they just needed to see who the others were.

There was an evil coming. Lucia just hoped that they found them all in time. Whoever was behind everything, knew what they were doing. She'd give them that, but that was all she was willing to give them.

"Why Aunt Lucia? I understand why you bond my powers, but how did you not know when my mother disappeared? "

"That, my dear niece I can't wait to find out. When I bond your powers, I tied them into your mother so that if anything happened, they would be returned to you."

"But mom died years ago. Shouldn't you have felt something? Things are not right...."

With her mind racing and her frustration growing, Ad could feel the warmth flowing down her body, could see the flames reaching from the tips of her fingers, trying to soothe her. The more emotion she had, the more the fire wanted to protect her. 'Just wait. Serina, just wait till I find you' was all Ad could think about.

"We will worry about why I didn't find out, later. Right now, we need to work on your control. If you want to defeat Serina, you're going to need all the strength you've got."

With her aunt's help, Adrianna knew that she could do anything. For the first time in a long time, she had family on her side and it felt good. Family, was what was going to give Adrianna her strength and help her to stop Serina. The more she practiced, the better she felt. Knowing that time didn't matter here, she focused on her magic. Learning to deepen her control, she continued to call fire forward to her. Just feeling the energy rush around her was outstanding. She felt more alive now than ever before. Taking a break, Ad wanted to see where her mother had grown up. Hoping her Aunt would show her, thinking there would be no harm in asking.

"Aunt Lucia, can you show me around, please? I would like to learn more about my mother's world; maybe it will help me discover more about my other half."

"There are those here that didn't know that your mother had a child. We best stay safe because we cannot draw unwanted attention to you. There are people here that felt your mother betrayed them when she chose to live in your realm, instead of fulfilling her duties here."

"Her duties here, you make her sound important."

"She was important. Very important. But there are people here, that if they found out about you, they would find you in your youth, and return you to take over your mothers' duties. Because of that we must be careful."

"Who exactly is she?"

"Let's just say that she has a special place amongst a very important family, and if certain members knew of you it would be all bad; and for now, that's enough about the subject.

Your mother's life will be become known to you when the time is right and not before."

Lucia hoped that it was going to be a long time watching as Adrianna fell to the ground, clutching her chest, Lucia rushed to help her.

As Adrianna laid there on the ground, she felt as if her heart was going to stop. Something was wrong she knew it, she had to get back. Taking a moment to recoup herself Ad knew that it was time to go, and Lucia knew too.

"I am going back with you Ad; you are going to need all the help that you can get. But I

can't jump alone, you need to take me with you." Lucia knew that there was more going on, she just wasn't sure if her niece was aware of it.

"I have never done that before. What if something goes wrong? I just found you, I can't lose you."

"You're not going to lose me don't worry. But it's going to take both of us to defeat Serina and free my mother. We must go now, and finish what she started all those years ago."

"But...."

"Just concentrate Ad. You can do it. Just hold my hand and we will go together."

Grasping her hand, taking deep breaths to steady her nerves. Concentrating now was more important than ever before. Everyone was counting on her, even if they didn't know it yet. Together they were no match for her sister.

While the world around her blurred out again for a moment, she could see her prison appear once again. The tightness in her chest began to release. Rubbing the part of her chest, where once a pain ravaged through, suddenly felt whole again. Calm removed the feeling of panic that was just there.

AWAKEN THE FLAMES

CHAPTER SEVENTEEN

"What do you mean we are only two floors above Serina?" Luc stood there with a puzzled look on his face.

"When we tried to locate you through the necklace Mary gave you, we realized just how close you were. With both Mary's and Serina's spells, they never knew of each other. Ad's close Luc, we just need to be smart about this."

"Smart, where's Mary. Paul, you would never leave someone behind, and by the look on Vince's face I can see something went wrong."

"Let's just say, when we find her, I'm sure that you are going to owe her big-time buddy."

As soon as we get your girlfriend, you better hurry up and find Vince's', even if he doesn't realize it yet. Because if he is anything like you are, we're going to be screwed."

Looking back and forth between Paul and Vince, Luc knew that after they saved Adrianna, their work was just beginning. He had a feeling they'd have to look for his cousin Sebastian as well. With nowhere to begin, it was going to be hard to find any of them. Serina was good, he just hoped that they were better.

To have never known she lived in the same building with Serina? Whatever Serina was up too was big. For magic that strong to be present and for neither of them to notice, something wasn't right. They didn't have time to figure that out now. That would come after they freed Adrianna. This was some magic that uncle Sal really needed to know about. Had Serina become that powerful? He didn't even want to spend time thinking about it. They needed to do something fast.

"So, we know where they are, what are we going to do?"

"We could always take the direct approach."

"What, walk up to the front door and ring the doorbell."

"Yea, because that's going to work."

"Not us, I have someone else in mind."

"If you mean..."

"You have a better idea, Luc because I don't." Looking between his friends, Paul knew that his idea would work. It had to; he was running out of time. The question was who was going to call Sal. And since he wasn't related, one of them could do it.

They both knew that Paul was right. No matter how much his uncle didn't want to see Serina at this moment, Ad's and Mary's life depended on it. They just needed him to distract Serina and they could do the rest.

#   #   #

Adrianna reappeared in her prison, only to find that her aunt wasn't with her. Not knowing what happened, but she also knew that she couldn't risk leaving again so soon. Aunt Lucia said that I left a shadow behind, but Ad wasn't entirely convinced. So many things could have happened. But she was sure that she returned at the same time she left. A quick glance around ensured that. Everyone was still asleep.

With all this power, Adrianna was lost on what to do. There was so much magic in her; feeling it coursing through her veins. There were so many factors that were going to come into play. She had to make sure that she saved not only herself now, but Luc's parents and her grandmother. As well as anyone else that Serina had trapped. Feeling the eeriness of the place closing in. Knowing that the longer she was here, the worse it would be.

Her mother always had a necklace she wore, but she hadn't seen it in years. It resembled the one that Serina was wearing. As if a light bulb went off, she suddenly had a sickening feeling who the other women trapped was. Not being able to see her from where she was. She couldn't be sure.

All Adrianna knew was that she needed to get that necklace back. Since she couldn't get it now, she'd have to go back to the past and too. Serina wasn't going to like it, but she knew where the perfect place to hide it was going to be. She had to be careful of who she told what to and why. Just enough clues so that when the time came, they'd know how to help her.

The question was now when to go back, and how to get the necklace without her mother knowing? This was going to be harder than she thought. If her mother saw her and started to question her, how was she going to cover? She couldn't risk running into herself;

but she'd be damned if she would let Serina get her grubby hands on it especially, since now that she had a way of preventing it.

If her mother discovered why she was really doing this, she might try and stop what has already happened. Adrianna had to make sure that she didn't change any of them outcomes.

She would give anything, to have her mother back in her life for the last year, but then she would have never learned about her father or met Luc. This was going to be harder than she first thought. Weren't the most important choice in life, always the hardest ones. She needed to hide it to kept it safe. How could she convince her mother to help her, and not reveal the whole truth?

A feeling of calm washed over her; she knew that someone was helping. Reminding her, to keep her cool. Maybe her aunt did make it through but was stuck in limbo somewhere. Considering that she was the only one in the frame, to begin with.

When to go back and get the necklace she had to think. She had to be sure of when. It couldn't be too far in the past. If she went too far her mother would spend years looking for it. She didn't want that to happen. The months before her mother died, she wasn't really wearing it that much. Just like a light bulb going off, Adrianna knew when she was going to go. She was going to have to go quickly.

Focusing on the day before her mother died, it wouldn't leave her time to look for it. If Serina had been the one that took it? That would have been when she did. Serina wasn't going to get her hands on it this time.

With some quick focusing, she was there. Luckily, she didn't look much different from that day. Knowing that on that day she wasn't home it would be the perfect time. Adrianna could feel herself moving through time. Life in slow motion again, not sure if she would ever get used to that aspect of it. As soon as her time came, she knew to materialize, and everything came into focus. Her aunt Lucia was right, the more she shifted, the easier it became.

"Hi, mom."

"Hey Ad, I thought you were going out with Mary tonight?"

"Yea, um... I forgot something so thought that I'd come back quickly." Hating lying to her mother, but it was the only way.

"I shouldn't be home too late. Just going for a bite and then will be back."

Running to her mother's room while she wasn't paying attention, knowing exactly where the necklace was. She hated doing this, but had to make sure that it was in a safe place. All she wanted to do was hug her mom and never let her go.

Tell her everything; explain all of it to her. Ad knew that she couldn't. Too many things in history would change. Ad couldn't live with that on her shoulders. Stuffing the necklace into her pocket, making a quick exit wasn't an option. There was something she had to do first. She couldn't change the future. However, knew the words that one day her mother would say that would give her strength.

"Okay, I'll see you when you get back."

"Alright, mommy. I love you, never forget that OK."

It wasn't something that Ad normally did, but she knew that it would be the last time she would see her mom. Leaving out the front door she returned to her time as quick as possible. Her eyes full of tears. Even knowing that the necklace would be safe, and it was for the best. If Serina was looking for it she wasn't going to find it.

Giving herself a few minutes to pull herself back together. Adrianna never realized how much she missed not saying goodbye to her mother, until that day. She had seen her in shifts before, but this one bothered her the most. Knowing that if she did not go now, she was going to run out of time. The sun would be up soon, and Serina would be back.

Shifting quickly again to go to Mary's, Ad needed to give her the necklace after Mary told her the truth, but before she was captured. It might not make sense to her friend now, but it would. Seeing her friend sit there in shock over how fast Ad learned to flash was funny, but Adrianna had to be quick about it.

"Mary, I need you to hold onto this for me, keep it safe, you'll know when to use it. I'm

counting on you. I'll explain later. I just need your help. Take this; it's my mother's necklace. I

saw it around Serina's neck. I went back to grab it. Figure out how to use it, it's the key to our freedom," being afraid of giving them too much information.

Emotions sometimes got in the way, and none of them needed that now. Before her friend could ask any questions, Adrianna shifted back to her own time. She needed to make one more trip before everything was set in motion.

Choosing to go back to Mary's on the proper time, she just didn't count on who she would see.

Mary sat there more confused than ever, "key to their freedom" she mumbled to herself.

CHAPTER EIGHTEEN

"Fine, I'll call him and tell him his daughter is bat shit crazy."

Luc was going to kill his dear cousin when all this was done. Sending off a quick text, Sal had been on standby since the whole thing started. Luc knew how he was feeling, he couldn't imagine how his uncle was staying so calm.

"Done, he should be here any second."

Knowing that this was not going to go over very well, Luc prepared for the worst. Uncle Sal wasn't going to like this, but he was their best chance at getting Adrianna back. No sooner he thought of Uncle, he was there in the room before them.

"Uncle Sal, before you say anything there is something you need to help us with.........."

Not even having a chance to finish his sentence, there in the room in front of him appeared Adrianna. As if they all noticed her at once, the room fell silent. Not wanting to believe his eyes. How was this even possible? How had she escaped Serina's? Luc ran over to hold her, not caring that her father was there at all; she was back and that's all he cared about. Holding her tightly in his arms, making sure that she was alright and nothing bad had happened to her. Not ever wanting to lose her again.

"Luc, how, what?"

"Ad, please say that you're OK? We've been so worried, how did you?"

"I didn't I can only stay a moment. If Serina knows that I'm gone, there is no telling what she will do. There is more than just my life at stake." Looking into his eyes, leaving him was the last thing she wanted, but she did have any other options.

"Luc let her finish. Ad, what are you doing here? How are you?"

"Ad....."

"Luc, I'll explain everything later, just get us out of there."

Feeling herself slowly fading out she noticed him 'Father....', then she found herself back where she had started. She didn't know how, but knew that it was her father. He was helping to find her. She just hoped Mary remembered about the necklace and figured out how to use it. Looking down at his chest, the necklace Mary had given him earlier began to glow.

Sal noticing the amulet around his nephew's neck, it had been the one he had given Adrianna's mother before she had left. He didn't know how Luc had it, but it was worth more than any of them known, it just needed to be with Adrianna. His mother gave it to Sebastian to bring to him years ago, she said he'd know who to give it too.

Feeling all his emotions that had built over the years trying to surface, Sal needed to gain control. He just couldn't believe that she had kept it. Sal had given it to Nina, shortly after they meet. It held the warmth of the sun, the strength of the wind, the power of the water, the closeness of earth, and the spirit of his undying love for her. It was so that she always knew that he cared.

She never knew the power that she held. Sal had never told her that it was charmed. How did Adrianna figure out its importance? The necklace had the purest of all magic in it. People would have given anything for its power. He gave it to Nina because he knew her to be pure, and she would always keep it safe.

Adrianna had given them the gift to freeing her, but there was going to be more to it than
just the necklace. He'd have to ask his Paul about the one he wore though, and how he had it. It was identical to his but held an emerald, and it wasn't a coincidence.

#   #   #

"NOOOOOOOOOOOOOOOOOOOOOO!!!!!!!!!!!" Serina scream echoed through the home, her energy vibrating everything around, the realm shifting off its axis for a mere moment.
Smiling to herself, Adrianna realized that Serina just noticed the missing necklace. Now all she needed was for Luc to figure it out.

As if on cue, Serina stormed into her trophy room. You could feel the anger radiating off her. She shouldn't have remembered having the necklace. But with the magic she used, anything was possible. Grabbing the frame on the top shelf, you knew that it wasn't going to go well.

"How did you do it?" Serina shaking the frame.

"Do what? What are you talking about?" The voice from the frame, Adrianna knew it.

It had been years but knew the second she heard the voice, that it was her mothers. She had to stay strong and not let on or everything will fall apart.

"Get the necklace, how did you take the necklace?"

"I didn't take the necklace you bitch, I'm trapped in here, how am I supposed to get out. You knew what I was before you put me in here. You knew that I couldn't get out. My brother was helping you; all this time and knew exactly what you were doing. Why don't you go ask him? He's the one who stole it, and gave it to you in the first place. Or are you no longer in my dear brother's plans?" Nina knew exactly who took the necklace and when, as the memories came flooding back to her from that day.

At the realization that her uncle was behind all this, Ad had to wonder if he knew the truth about her. Or did he just figure that she had no powers and wasn't worth the trouble. That's why her aunt didn't want her to leave the garden. If her uncle knew that she had discovered the truth, she wouldn't be safe. Her gut always told her not to trust him, and was glad that she listened. Slamming the frame back down on the shelf, Serina left the room. Knowing that she wasn't going to get the answers she wanted, only building her frustration more. The only problem was that she didn't put the frame back where she got it from. Instead, she put it beside Luc's parents, and Ad had the perfect view of her mother.

"Mommy?" Adrianna said as if she were a lost child. After realizing her mother had been captured, and seeing her alive and well, emotions overwhelmed her. Flames cocooning around her to protect her from the emotional turmoil she was feeling. Her family was going to be complete for the first time in her life.

As if slowly recognizing the voice, Ad's mother turned stared back at her daughter for the first time in years. She looked the same as the day in the kitchen when Adrianna had taken the necklace. Nina knew her daughter would have only taken it if she was in dire need. Seeing her daughter captured after keeping her secret, she had so many questions, but wanting nothing more than to hold Adrianna in her arms.

"How? How did she?"

"Don't, she doesn't know who I am, and we're trying to keep it that way. Are you alright?"

"Yes, Adrianna, I'm fine. But what's going on. And why did you take my necklace that day?"

"You knew I took it."

"Ad, you called me mommy and said I love you. And you had different clothes since you had left five minutes earlier. I knew that it had to be for a good reason so I never questioned you."

"Why didn't you tell me what we were?"

"Your uncle isn't the nicest member of the family. All he knew was that because your father was mortal, and you never received any of our powers. He didn't know that I had

them bound. If he believed that you were human, you were safe from his reach. He would stop at nothing if he knew the truth."

"Yea, but a little forewarning would have been nice. But I had some help with that."

Her mom didn't need to know about her father yet, they had enough going on.

"I'm so sorry Adrianna. I've missed you so much."

"I missed you mom." Ad knew that Luc's parent and her grandmother could hear them. They'd let them have their moment which was nice.

"Mom, how does the necklace work? How can we get out?"

"You can't leave the frame, it's no use."

"I can, Serina doesn't know what I am. She thinks I'm human. She is just trying to punish someone I care about. I've left and can again. Just tell me how to use them necklace."

"I'm not sure. But whatever it is, Serina wanted enough to cause all these terrible things.

Someone gave it to me a long time ago, I just can't remember who. I knew enough

that it had to be kept safe."

Adrianna knew that the person had to be her father. Her mom couldn't remember because of whatever Serina and her uncle had done. That's why Lucia was stuck in between. She must have felt its power, so she stayed hidden. She could hear her aunt whispering in her ear. 'It just has to be close. Magic isn't about tricks Adrianna, it about feeling. When you feel the true power, it will set you free. Family works the best. I'm here for you niece.' Feeling comforted by her aunt, she knew she needed some answers before they escaped, she needed some information from her mother.

"Mom, why didn't you stay with dad?"

"Ad, really now isn't the best time."

"No, now is a perfect time."

"He wanted to be with me forever and I couldn't. He would have aged, and I wouldn't have."

"But, if you could go back, and have just a short amount of time, would you? Do you remember much about that time?"

"No, I don't remember much. I remember him. His face gets clearer each day. But the details are all fuzzy, but that has only been in the last few days. And yes, I wish I would have promised him forever." That was the one thing that Ad's mom would go back and change as soon as she had a chance.

"So, do it, do it now. Even if it means he doesn't hear it, you know that you said it, even

if we don't get out of here." She needed her mom to say the words. Her father would feel it, and she was counting on it.

"I promise forever, to my one love."

Ad's mom had a feeling of empowerment wash over her. She didn't know why, but knew that she would be safe. Her daughter was up to something, she showed a confidence that she had never seen

239

before. Nina was proud of the woman Adrianna had become, and regretted the time they were apart, and would spend a lifetime making it up to her.

"Okay mom, now I have to go somewhere. Just stall Serina if she comes back before I do."

"But where...." But it was too late, she was already gone.

#   #   #

"Ad, you're back."

"Father" Seeing her dad holding himself up for support, Ad rushed over to his side.

"Adrianna, I'm fine really. I am so glad to finally meet you, my daughter."

"No offense but, we can save that for later. Luc, do you have the necklace."

"I just gave it to your dad."

"Dad put it in your pocket so Serina doesn't see it."

"Why? What's going on?" Luc was getting frustrated because things were happening so quickly. He couldn't believe how fast Adrianna learned how to flash.

"Luc, dad, and whoever you are over there."

"Paul and Vince."

"OK, and guys. Serina is weakened a bit since I took the necklace and gave it to Mary, but apparently, you have it now and Mary is missing. Dad, you must go down there and

get her to let you in. We are in a back room somewhere, we're in frames. And that the necklace can undo her spell. But she is getting angry and we're running out of time. She has...." looking at her father, she knew that he understood.

"You can count on me." Sal had lost Nina once before, and wasn't going to let it happen again.

"Luc, don't worry, I'll be fine, just get Serina and get them out of the frames. Dad will know what to do."

Before Luc could say anything, she was gone. He was almost sorry that he told her about flashing. If she was going to keep this up, he was going to go crazy.

Emerging back in her prison, her mother still looking to her for answers. Together they

could conquer anything. It would be too easy for everything to fall apart if something went

wrong. It was more than just her life at stake. Looking to her family, Adrianna knew they held

the strength she needed to free them all.

"Christina, how many of us are in here. There are the two of you, me, mom and the old woman. Is there anyone else?"

"No, that's it."

"Christina, we need to get Serina in here? She thinks I'm mortal and doesn't know I can get out. We have to do this now."

"Are you nuts? She's already pissed off...."

"Christina, help is coming and is closer than you think. It's now or never. If we all want to be free, we have to work together."

"Ad, what do you need us to do?"

"Mom, you get the old woman out of here and take her to your realm. Christina, you and Charles go with mom. I'll be right behind you. Don't worry."

"Lucia, wherever you are in here help mom with your mother, make sure they all get to safety."

"Why do I have the feeling I'm missing something daughter?"

"Because you are, and it's safer that way. Trust me. I just got you back and am not going

to lose you again. Stay in the garden with Lucia, and don't go into the city. Promise

me."

"I promise. Till I see you again. I love you, Adrianna."

"Love you too mom, now get ready. You're only going to have a few moments to leave.

Is everyone ready?"

With reluctant yes' from everyone, they all knew what they had to do. Hoping that her

Aunt Lucia heard what she said and go back with them. She knew that things were going to get interesting very soon. Adrianna was hoping for the best. Everyone's life depended on her. She

just needed to be patient and wait for her father.

It didn't surprise her that Luc and her dad were working together. When he finally knows

what her darling sister was up to; shit hitting the fan was going to be the least of Serina's worries.

He didn't seem like the type of guy that you wanted to piss off, even on a good day.

She didn't really peg her father as the all-forgiving type. In cases of unknowing accidents, yes; but purely premeditated insanity was not going to be one of them. Adrianna could see why Sal kept her a secret from her sister. The woman was off her rocker. Hell, the rocker broke years ago.

Beginning to hear some commotion in the other room, she knew the time to put the plan into action was going to be any moment. The second she saw her mom shift out of the frame; she knew that it was on.

"Take them and get out of here now!"

"Be safe Adrianna."

"I will mom, just go. I can't stop Serina if I have to worry about the four of you." No sooner then she said it, they all vanished.

Adrianna took a moment to view the room she was in. There were so many frames, all were empty for the moment, but how long had they held silent prisoners. Not wanting to take any chances, she grabbed her grandmother's frame and put it aside.

The rest she quickly packed up and flashed back to her house. She had to make sure that they were empty before they were destroyed. Ad didn't want anyone who was innocent to get hurt any more than they already had.

She was sure that once word was out about what Serina had been up to, there would be more than just her family looking to get even. Remembering a memory as a child, and thinking everyone were all just pieces in a big doll house. That's exactly how her sister treated them. She was soon to become the doll in her own house. Ad hoped that she would enjoy it just as much as her victims did.

Returning to the room, she grabbed her grandmother's prison. If it was strong enough to hold her grandmother, then it had to be strong enough to hold Serina. Tucking it the back of her jeans, it would be ready for quick access. It was now or never.

With all the yelling and screaming going on the room, Serina wasn't aware that there was anyone else there besides her, and her father.

"How could you? You miserable, selfish child."

"Child! How dare you call me child, I'm over 450 years old."

"When you act the way, you've been acting, a child suits you just fine."

"I am the way I am because of you! How could you!!"

244

"How could I what? Get duped by that bitch of a mother of yours. She knew exactly what she did, and you want to blame me. You, ungrateful brat! I gave you everything. How long have you been here for, it's been centuries since you've shown your face to anyone."

"I don't need you in my life! How did you find me? I'm the one the elders talked about. No one can touch me." Smugly she snapped at him.

Realizing that Adrianna was in the room, Sal carefully watched his body movements. He had to make sure that Serina didn't see her. With Luc, Vince, and Paul suddenly appearing in the room, it was the distraction that he needed.

"You!"

"Hello Serina, I warned you not to mess with us didn't we. You should have listened."

"I thought I took care of you before." With that Serina hurled another blast of energy at Vince. Adrianna quickly captured it with her flame.

Taking Serina by surprise. Playing with the fire in the palm of her hands, watching Serina trying to figure out what was going on. Ad knew better, but truly wanted to see what her sister was capable of.

Letting the flames lick the insides of her wrist, and allowing it to change shape, she was prepared for Serina's next move. Serina forced a blast of energy at her, so strong that the very room shook. What her sister didn't expect was for Adrianna to absorb it.

"You can do that all day Serina; it's not going to get you anywhere. After everything you've done, did you really think I would just roll over?"

"Roll over would be smart for someone as dumb as you. My fault for underestimating you, and thinking you mortal. Trust me that won't happen again." Focusing all her powers, Serina needed to make a direct hit.

With Luc, her father and the others were staring at her, Adrianna needed to prove a point. She needed Serina to know that no matter what she would try, that Adrianna would always be there to stop her. That for everything bad, there was a good. Serina could hurl fire at her all day. It made her stronger using Serina power to amplify her own.

Standing there, realizing nothing was working, she needed to escape. Whoever this Holly was, she was strong and would be dealt with Serina thought to herself, no one did this and got away with it, she'd make sure.

As if reading her mind, Ad let her fire flow through her and wrap around Serina, forcing her to remain. Adrianna positioned herself close enough to Serina; she knew the frame would work.

"Hey sis, how about you look over here."

"Who the?" As the words sunk in, the woman in the frame? Her father? A sister? As Serina was sucked into the frame, she realized the trouble she had gotten herself into.

Looking through the frame and seeing Holly staring back. It couldn't be. Realizing after all these years that she wasn't the one.

246

She wasn't destined to be great. That her father kept a secret from her. A sister. How did she miss that there was a child?

"You thought you were so smart, didn't you? Making my mother, leave our father. But what you didn't know I was part of the package. He never told you about me, did he?"

"No, you can't?"

"Oh, yes I can. You took my father away from me and then my mother. You just never knew about me. See, Mary kept me safe. Hid me from you, but you're not the one Serina. You're not the powerful one. You never counted on dad having another daughter."

"When I get..."

"You wont, and when I find my brother, I'm sure he will have a few words for you. By the way, the name is Adrianna. I suggest that you remember it. Also, Luc is mine so get over it."

"No, you can't have him." Serina was boiling over, all her work. Everything ripped apart. She was trapped. And she knew the spell on this frame; it wouldn't be broken easily. It was for her grandmother. If it was strong enough to keep her in it, there was no hope.

"What you did to him, his parents, my mother, your father, our brother......do you honestly, think anyone in their right mind would help you after this? And Mary, when I find her, you are going to wish you were never born!" Seeing the recognition on Luc's face, Ad knew that she had to tell him. Passing the frame to her father; she knew that Serina would be put in a safe place. No-one would have to worry about Serina for a long time.

Rushing over to give Luc a huge hug, she was so glad to be back in his arms. There was nowhere else in the world she would rather be. Safe and secure in the arms of the man she loved. It didn't matter if they only knew each other for a short time. She could feel the fire warming and surrounding her.

"Do you want to go see your mom and dad? They have some news for you as well."

"Have I told you today that I love you Ad, and yes. You can explain the whole fire, glowing thing to me later."

Easing her down so her feet touched the ground, not wanting to break apart from her. With her head tucked under his chin, he wasn't sure if he'd be the one protecting her, or she him. The one thing he knew was that she wasn't going to leave his side again.

"Adrianna before you two go, can I have a moment."

Letting herself slip from Luc's arms, reaching for his hand wanting to keep contact with him. Stepping closer to her father, she knew that her life was going to be back on track. She had an eternity to get to know her family.

"I want to give you this back; it's your mothers necklace. I know how much it means to you. Just make sure she gets it." Sal was holding the necklace in his hand.

"I think she would rather get it back from you," she said as she closed his fingers gently around it.

"I'll have her back in a few; just meet us at my house." Placing a small kiss on her father's cheek, stepping back to Luc, squeezed his hand and then was gone.

It was the first contact she had with her father. As he raised his hand to his cheek, cherishing the moment. He had his daughter back and would get a chance to know her. The years of searching were over.

Looking at the frame in his hand, part of him was grateful for Serina bringing them together so quickly. The other part will make her pay for destroying the world he could have had.

"Serina, I have a nice shelf for you, where no one is going to find you."

"But, dad, you can't."

"You took my life, Sebastian's and Nina's life away from me. Made me miss Adrianna growing up. My mother and apparently, Luc's parents as well. You think I'm going to let you cause havoc again? Enjoy your prison daughter, because you're not going to ever see the outside world again."

Flashing out and back to his house, Sal went to the basement and unlocked his safe. Serina would have no way out. Not only was the frame charmed, but the safe was as well. He had made sure of its security. Having hired only trusted contractors, nothing could ever be safe enough.

Closing the door, locking it behind him. He knew the world would be safe from his daughter. The trouble the women stirred up was unbelievable. Unaware of the shadows behind him, he left the basement; he went to wait for Adrianna and the rest of his family back at her house. He was sure this was a week; he wasn't going to forget. He had his daughter back and Nina as well. Sal had felt when Nina had promised forever to him. Knew that it was what she wanted. He just hoped that she liked the immortality package that came along with it.

Rubbing his chest where his heart was, he was whole again for the first time in years. Looking around at the quaintness of his daughter's home, he could tell that she had a loving childhood. The pictures on the walls spoke volumes. He may have missed the first years of her life, but he would spend eternity getting to know the wonderful woman she had become.

CHAPTER NINETEEN

Taking Luc to her mother's realm was going to be interesting. First to learn that his parents were alive and had been trapped them for years. Then the fact she could jump through time. She hoped that he could deal with everything all at once.

Adrianna just couldn't wait to see her mother again. She was happy that her mom figured out what she had said on her last visit. How her mother was going to react to everything else was another story. Just to have her back and home with her was more than she ever could have asked for.

"Mom."

"Adrianna, you're alright. I was so worried."

"It's OK mom, I'm just glad that I have you back."

Nina wrapped her arms around her daughter, she could feel all her bottled-up emotions coming to the surface. Too finally have her back with her after so many years. They would have so much catching up to do. Tears streaming down her cheeks unable to see through the haze nothing had ever felt so wonderful.

"Mom, I missed you so much...." She managed to get out between sobs.

"Adrianna, it's alright. Don't cry, I'm here." Nina said as she brushed the tears off her daughter's face. Looking at her and seeing how much she had matured over the years.

"It's alright. Mom, we're together now." She said holding her mother close and not wanting to let her go as if she was a little girl holding on to her favorite toy.

Having her mother hold her in her arms was more that Adrianna could have ever wished for. They would not be separated again. She'd make sure of it. All those lost years, her having to grow up faster than she needed to. Serina was behind them now. Her father was going to make sure of that. If anyone knew what to do with that woman her dad would. Adrianna was sure that her grandmother had something special in store for her as well.

Not wanting to part from her mother, knowing that her father was waiting at her place for them. Ad knew that her father would be worried about them being gone for so long. Even though it was mere minutes, compared to the lifetime of waiting; but her parents deserved to see each other. Her mother needed to learn the truth about everything.

They had so much to sort out. So much that they didn't know about each other; but,
now was their time. She was going to make sure that no one disturbed them. They needed to heal from the pain Serina inflicted on them. They might never get back the time they had been torn apart, but now they would have a lifetime to make up for it.

More years than either of them would truly know what to do with. Seeing her grandmother, and spotting her aunt Lucia there as well. Looking over her mother's shoulder, she could see Lucia embracing her mother as well. All this turmoil brought on by her sister, and that she would never forget. She was going to have to explain a lot to her mom, by that could wait. That being a lot longer now that she knew they were immortal.

"Ad, I'm sorry, I should have told you."

"It's OK mom. I remembered something from when I was a child, and Lucia helped me with the rest; as well as Christina and Charles."

"It's no excuse if I told you; you would have been more prepared. Serina knew what I was because of my brother and used a cursed frame, so I was trapped."

"Mom, go back to our house and I'll meet you there. I'll be right behind you. I'm just going to check on everyone and bring them back to our realm. Or close enough that they can get there themselves."

Trying to figure out why her daughter was rushing her, but Nina knew that she would find out soon enough. She shifted herself back to the present back to her home. Turning, Adrianna kneeled beside her grandmother. A person she never dreamed of having in her life. The lessons and stories she could learn from her. To have such a large family from being alone. Looking at the woman staring back at her; Adrianna wondered if her grandmother knew what would happen all along?

"Grandmother are you alright?"

"Yes, dear I am." Giving her grandmother a hug for the first time. Adrianna had the family she had always longed for; and would fight to make sure that nothing ever happened to it again.

"You are a brave child, Adrianna, and I'm honored to call you my grand-daughter. You have more power than you know, but that will come in time. Once all is back too normal, we will have a chat the two of us. I will tell you everything you need to know. The spirits choose wisely when they gifted you. You are strong and deserve the fire they bestowed upon you. Now go my dear, Lucia is going to take me home to rest and recoup. The next time I see you I shall be back to my old self. Much love grand-daughter."

"I look forward to seeing you again and thank you." Life was going to be fun. Leaving her

grandmother and Aunt, she made her way over to Luc and his parents.

Having Adrianna by his side, Luc didn't care where he was. He had her back and that was what mattered. Seeing his parents standing there in front of him, after being thought lost for so many years. Instead, it had been Serina who caused all their pain.

Having been over three hundred years, he understood how Adrianna felt moments before

with her mother. Being so young when they vanished, with no knowledge of where they went. It all made sense. How one woman could be so cold and calculating was beyond him.

"Luc!" Christina shouted as she ran over to him, and he wasn't going to let her go.

"Mom...." As Adrianna watched Charles follow Christina over to Luc, Ad knew that they needed to talk. There was so much Christina had to catch him up on. Serina reaped havoc in their lives so much, he just never realized or would have thought her capable of taking his parents.

He was just glad that they were back, and they were safe. Sal had been great, but some days he just wanted his family. Letting his mother coddle him like a child, he knew that she had a lot to say. He just wasn't prepared for all the facts that she gave. He would do everything in his power to set things right.

"I have a brother, Ad, I have a brother. We have to...." Tears filling his eyes over run by emotions.

"I know. We will find him. Let's go home and we can figure out a plan from there. We also have to find Mary and Sebastian as well."

First getting his parents settled over at Mary's place. Being sure she wouldn't mind; they truly needed a good night's sleep. He made sure to show them all the modern-day wonders that they weren't accustomed to. Picking Ad up in his arms, he wasn't going to ever let her go. Anything they did, they were going to do together from now on. He was stronger with her by his side, she was the other half of his heart, he had known it from the first second, he saw her.

"Thank you for all of this Adrianna, it means the world to us. Luc's place is beside you right now. Go see your parents we will meet up in a few hours." Giving Adrianna a hug, she was so grateful for her bringing the family back together. When they find Mateo, their family will be whole again.

"Thank you, Christina."

She took Luc's in her arms, and wrapped him around her, and wasn't about to let go. She hoped that her father and mother were going to be alright. Having both alive and in her life, was more than she could have asked for.

#   #   #

Finding herself back at home, Nina just needed a minute to absorb everything that happened. It was a welcoming feeling like being home. How one woman could be so cruel was beyond her. Like a weight had been lifted, all Nina's memories came flooding back. She had a name to the face that haunted her dreams for years. Serina's spell on her had finally been broken.

Unable to believe his eyes Sal stood there. It was Nina, out of thin air, there, in front of him. Sal had spent years and all his resources looking for her. Not even considering that Serina was behind it. The thought just made his blood boil. Realizing that Nina didn't see him, Sal just wanted to rush up to her, and it took everything for him not to. He knew that she needed a few moments. She had been put through so much over the last few years.

Walking around and checking out her surrounding, Nina knew what she had to do. She needed to go back and talk to Sal one more time. So much had changed, but she needed him to know about Ad so he could protect her. She didn't care about changing fate, but she knew that Ad would be looked after.

Turning around about to shift. There he was standing in front of her. Her, Sal, right there; waiting for her. Emotions overtaking her, her heartbeat increasing as she heard its deafening pounding in her chest; blinking to see past the tears that were filling her eyes. How did she wonder? She didn't understand. Feeling her legs weakening beneath her, Sal grabbing her for support as she collapsed towards the floor. Nina knew they would be alright. She just had to tell him about herself, and was relieved that Ad had found her father. Pulling him through time was breaking the rules, she had a chance to make things right, at that moment she didn't care.

"Nina, it's OK, relax."

"Sal, but? How?"

"Just rest, everything will be fine." Leaning down and placing a kiss on her lips, Sal wasn't going to let her go this time, no matter what. He waited for the moment for so long that nothing was going to ruin it for either of them.

Letting him hold her, she knew that she had some time. She couldn't figure why he wasn't freaked out about seeing her suddenly appear. How did he know she would be there? How had they found each other after so much time had passed? Would he be able to accept her for who she was?

So many questions came flooding to her. Not understanding the motivation behind leaving him. She would never have done that willingly. She was going to tell him about herself, she was missing something she was sure of it.

"Sal, really, there is something that.........."

"Whatever it is it can wait. I've waited over a century for this moment, and I'm not going to let anything ruin it. You are the love of my life, Nina. You blessed us with a beautiful baby girl. I'm sorry for everything my daughter put you, and us through. I'll spend every day trying to make it up to you. I should have realized sooner, then none of this would have happened. At least now your finally my wife so I have years to make it up to you."

"But, you? Me? How? What's going on? And why do you still look the same as you

did all those years ago? Why do I feel like I'm missing something that I shouldn't be?

Wife?" Pausing for a moment, she let the words sink in. Something she had always wished for,

but didn't think would happen.

"I begged you to promise me forever and marry me. I wanted nothing more. I couldn't give you my immortality or tell you about it, until you pledged forever. When Luc gave me the necklace, I could sense you. Didn't fully understand it until you made you pledge. Then I could feel that you were near. When you appeared in front of me....it was like my whole world opened into a new beginning. Once you made your pledge, I was able to gift you with immortality."

"Um......Sal, darling; you could not have gifted me with immortality, because I am already an immortal. All these years, I felt like I had kept a secret from you, yet, you had the same secret." Silently laughing to herself. They were more alike than either of them knew.

Telling him about her and who she was and listening to his story as well. Realizing if they were only honest in the first place, none of this may have happened. But, everything in life happens for a reason. Fate and Destiny had plans for how the world would play out. Maybe trusting in them was the real answer.

"A time shifter, well that explains how our daughter could jump around pretty fast. But her witch half is really going to need some work. And why it took a hundred years to find her."

"Witch half? I think now that our daughter is immortal; we will have a lifetime of teaching ahead of us. That reminds me of the young witchling I saved years ago. There was someone after Lucia, so I hid her, and she's been protected ever since. She whipped up the best windstorms when she was mad though."

"Lucia? You said you saved a Lucia?"

"Yes, when I found her, she kept saying that there was someone chasing her. That she needed help. When Adrianna discovered how to jump when she was little, I had Lucia bind her powers. She had a knack for causing things to burn though. I guess that would have been her witch half, now a lot of things make sense."

"Lucia, she is my sister. She probably sensed Adrianna's special talents and wanted to keep her safc. Lucia is very special. And I've seen our daughter talent for fire. She is going to have a lot on her plate.

I'll tell you about our history later. Right now, I just want to hold you in my arms." Gazing into her eyes after being separated for years, he brushed his lips over hers and lost himself. Sal gathered Nina up in his arms and held her and wasn't going to let her go.

"Mom!" Seeing her mother on the floor in her father arms, she rushed over. "Dad, what's wrong. Is she alright?"

"Adrianna, I'm fine, just how? Why?"

"It's alright mom, we'll explain everything. But you and dad can be together now, it's OK, you don't have to worry."

Helping her dad get her mom to the couch, Ad and her father began to fill her mother in on everything that was going on. They could finally be a family.

With Luc sitting on the couch beside her, Adrianna finally knew that this was what it was like to be loved and wanted that this feeling was going to last forever. She had spent the last years alone, and in a matter of minutes she had more family than she could have ever dreamed of.

"So, Luc, do you have something to tell my daughter." With the look that Sal was giving him, Luc knew that he was going to have to tell Ad. He had to be the one to tell her but didn't know how she would react.

"Ad, can we go somewhere and talk for a few minutes, just the two of us. It will give

your mom and dad a chance to catch up."

Looking at her parents, seeing how happy they were just to be with each other she smiled.

It was an image she would keep with her forever, nodding to Luc to let him know it was alright. Holding her in his arms, smiling down, he flashed them back to his apartment.

"Ad, I have something to tell you, and I don't know how you're going to take it."

"Take what Luc?" She said coyly knowing full well what was going on, but wanting to enjoy the moment. Watching as he fidgeted trying to think of the right words to say just endeared himself more to her.

"Remember how I asked you if you would be with me forever, well, there was more to it than that."

"More.......like what?" She asked with a smug smile on her face.

"You're the one I want to spend the rest of my life with. In our ways, it's kind of saying that.... we're, ah......married." Looking at her and waiting for a response, his nerves were on edge; she just stood there for a moment and didn't say anything. He knew that he would do it all over again if he had to, she was one woman he wasn't willing to live without.

Bringing herself closer to him Adrianna snaked her arms around the back of his neck, and passionately capturing his lips. If it hadn't been for him, she wouldn't have her entire family back. With her lips gently making a path along his jaw towards the side of his face, she breathlessly whispered into his ear "There is no one that I would rather spend all eternity with than you."

Grabbing and lifting her, into his arms. Resting his forehead on her and staring deep into the depths of her eyes he knew this was what fate had in store for them. They were starting a

life together, and he couldn't be happier.

"We should go back and tell your parents...your dad figured it out, but your mom...."

"Luc, they haven't seen each other in a hundred years, I think they should be alright. There

is something else I would rather be doing right now anyway."

Adrianna leaned in to kiss him, just wanting to be in his arms, lifting her body so her legs hugged his waste, pulling him closer to her.

"Tomorrow, we are going to have to start putting together a plan to look for everyone."

Feeling bad for enjoying the moment when Mary and her brother was still missing Adrianna was torn.

"Ad, tomorrow can wait. Right now, I'm just going to devour my wife."

A sly smile spread across her face. Being married to him was going to be great.

EPILOGUE

After searching for weeks, they still hadn't found a trace of Mary. Serina could have sent
her anywhere; they didn't even know where to begin. They tried everything they could think of,
consulted oracles, witches, even psychics on the corners. But nothing had turned up. Just cryptic messages they couldn't make any sense of.

Vince had been growing frustrated by the minute and Luc hated seeing his friend in that
state. He had been mere days without Adrianna and it was driving him crazy. Vince was going on six weeks, crazy wasn't the word for it. He knew that Mary was his, and wasn't going to let
anything stop him from getting her back.

Just when they thought they found something or sense something everything would change. If Serina did have help; they needed to find out who it was. Adrianna decided to consult with Mary's sister Elena, even with Luc protesting. She had already lost her husband which had slowly driven her crazy, but the loss of her sister might put her over the edge.

When they reached Elena's house, she was semi-coherent, but just kept babbling about the water. Her parents said she had been like that since he disappeared. Completely fine until she was near water and then she would break down and begin to cry. Elena would sit there, stare into the depths. Looking out, reaching out, trying to contact her lost love. Adrianna's heart broke watching her. Finding her brother would bring her peace, and make Elena whole again.

Since they weren't getting the answers they needed, Luc pushed Adrianna to take a break. They needed to re-focus and concentrate. All the stress and she was going to burn herself out. He understood her stress with Mary became trapped trying to free Adrianna. However, she wasn't going to be any good to any of them unless she was energized. He had to push her to go to the beach just to relax.

"Luc, we shouldn't be here, we should be looking for Mary. For Sebastian........."

"I know, but right now you're not good to any of them, you search all day, and then you're busy

all night." He said with a sly smile across his face. In the six weeks since Adrianna found out the

truth about them being married, he had promised to make it up to her and did repeatedly.

"I'm busy all night with you, so that doesn't count." She said back playfully.

As they walked along the beach, Adrianna kept thinking she was missing something. As the water lapped her feet, and she gazed out into the deeps she would envision her friend, only wishing she knew how to help her.

#   #   #

Trying to figure out how Sebastian had lived in his prison for so long. Staring back at the people she cared about and not being able to talk to them   As Mary and Sebastian walked along the water following Luc and Adrianna, she just wished they could see them, how close they really were. Feeling the waves hitting her feet harder, she looked to Sebastian.

"What?"

"You know what. Stop doing that can it never be just a nice day at the beach since were stuck here. You're the one who wanted to follow them to the beach today." Mary would have rather

been seeing what Vince was doing instead of spending her day at the beach.

"Mary, you can't follow him around all the time, it'll make him crazy. Look at all those years I

spent trying to get through to your sister. She's fine and the certain things remind her of me and

then she starts to cry. I used to love it when she came to the beach and walked in the water.

Now she won't even come near it."

"Wait, what did you say?" As if a light bulb was going off in Mary's head, she had an idea. But it couldn't be that easy, could it? She thought to herself.

"Your sister's crazy?"

"No, you dumbass, about the beach?"

"She used to come to the beach to relax and try and forget, I'd walk beside her by the water. She would always leave in tears and eventually stopped coming."

He could see the wheels turning in Mary's head. She was thinking of something. Watching as the sun slowly began to set, and seeing Adrianna starting a small fire on the beach she looked to Sebastian.

"What can you do?"

"Nothing I couldn't do anything...."

"Not could, CAN. What can you do? Adrianna can control fire, Serina has crazy down pat; can

you do anything?"

"Yea, why? I can control water."

"Water, you control water?"

"Yea, so."

Pacing back and forth for a few minutes, it couldn't be that easy, could it. She needed Adrianna to get to the water to see if her theory would work.

"Sebastian, come with me, we need to go into the water."

"Why?" Over the years whenever Mary got that look in her eyes something always happened.

"We may be stuck, but I think I know a way to get a message through. You said Elena would

always leave the beach in tears. She would see your reflection in the water, but it wasn't a reflection, it was you. You may be trapped, but she could still see you when you were with your

element."

"What are you talking about?'

"Just come with me."

Dragging him to the lake and making him stand on the edge. If they held hands and stood in the same place as Adrianna maybe, just maybe she would be able to see them. Her plan had to work. There had to be a way out of this realm. Grabbing Adrianna to his side and swinging her over his shoulder Luc had other plans while they were at the beach. Walking towards the water with the sounds of Adrianna's giggles over his shoulder, he felt complete.

"Luc put me down!"

"Not yet, were not deep enough."

"No Luc put me down now." Putting her down in the water trying to see what she was doing.

Squatting closer to the water, Adrianna gazed deeply in not wanting to believe her eyes.

"What are you looking at?"

"It's Mary and a man, come look."

As he stood beside his wife and gazed into the water, he could see what she was looking at. It was Mary and Sebastian looking back at them. Their only question was how to get them from where ever they were.........

AWAKEN THE FLAMES

Made in the USA
Monee, IL
25 April 2021